A story of hope and passion, based on historical fact

AN IRISHMAN'S HOME

TERENCE KEAREY

MEREO

Mereo Books

2nd Floor, 6-8 Dyer Street, Cirencester, Gloucestershire, GL7 2PF
An imprint of Memoirs Books. www.mereobooks.com
and www.memoirsbooks.co.uk

An Irishman's Home
ISBN: 978-1-86151-819-4

First published in Great Britain in 2022
by Mereo Books, an imprint of Memoirs Books.

A CIP catalogue record for this book is available from the British Library.

The address for Memoirs Books can be
found at www.mereobooks.com

Mereo Books Ltd. Reg. No. 12157152

Typeset in 12/19pt Sabon
by Wiltshire Associates.
Printed and bound in Great Britain

To Stan

Previous books by Terence Kearey:

Safeguard Our Flank

A Glance in the Mirror

History, Heroism and Home

A Distance Travelled

A Changing World

Country Ways

The deckhand stands with rope in hand
The tide is turning – there's no band.
Thomas grasps the handrail, grips his bag
And marches up the swaying plank.
Now firm of foot – he stands at mast.
He dwells on life – on family's past.
The tenant's rent and tithe is due.
Tales of many… which are true.
He's served his time with metal ore
He's had enough of being poor.
London calls – he hears the blast
His head is down – to take the task.
Now, read of what he plans, and how he fares
To find his love, the one who cares?
The story's true – there was a man
Who left his home to make his way?
To find a job and room to stay.
He chanced upon a sweet young lass
Her love, he knew, he couldn't pass.
They made a home, and one night too
They gave their love and made their jewel.

Contents

The Kearey Clan

INTRODUCTION

My hereditary descent is from Thomas Kearey, my Irish great-great-grandfather, who appears in the 1851 London census as aged 60. The census records Thomas as being married to Ester Pepler, then aged 55, giving his occupation as a gold and silver smelter, and later as a refiner. In 1851 Thomas and Ester were residents of 20 North Row, Earls Court, in the Royal Borough of Kensington. When Thomas died in 1860 aged 70, he lived at 3 Nassau Street, which stretches from the A5204 to Riding Out Street, close to Broad Street station.

His description of having been born in Ireland in 1791 allows me to apply for a Grant of Arms for my descendants, from the Chief Herald of Ireland, a long-standing wish to link my Gaelic family connections with the past, to confirm all the necessary distinctions that three generations of arms have been used for at least 100 years. This need, perhaps obsession, has driven me to record as much as I can about my life and times – for my children's sake, as much as my own, and about the Kearey line in London, begun by Thomas. A final chapter on the Grant of Arms appears at the end of this book.

The Herald of Ireland later stated when answering my application: "From a heraldic point of view, based on the information to hand, I would suggest that a new Grant of Arms may make reference in some way to the generally accepted origin of the name Kearey in the Irish word 'ciar' used in the Gaelic surname of O'Ciardha. Combining this with heraldic devices may tell the story of your own immediate family starting from Thomas born in 1791. In that way, include your 'family arms' in the wider context of the name."

The Course of Irish History states: "The earlier, non-Indo-European, population survived under Celtic control. One group in particular, known as the P-Celtic or as Cruithni, survived into historical times as the Picts, or 'painted people' of Scotland. The Cruithni were numerous in Ulster, in family groups in Leinster and the Ciarraighe Tribes of Connacht."

The migrating Neolithic people, to be known as Celts, in 500 BC, were a population with a common culture and language. The Collins Irish Dictionary definition of 'ciar' is swarthy, and could be interpreted as either sun-tanned or painted brown (the description of Picts, given as 'painted people). However, in many official references 'ciar' is described as black or grey. The latest discoveries of man's occupation of the Scottish Isles make another link in the chain of tribal occupation.

O'Ciardha (pronounced O'Ceary or O'Keary) was the family Gaelic name handed down from ancient times, which continues to this day. The Irish language borrowed Latinized English, letters, words and sayings, to change Ceary and Cary, and to use 'K' and 'ey,' forming a recognisable and familiar link to the 'English' usage of the language rather than Gaelic. This change had to be sanctioned by the greater O'Ciardha family, recognising that this could be considered yet another loss to clan heritage.

I idly look at a book of Irish history on my desk and flick through its pages; its subjects follow exactly my confusion as I write family history. Here are just four: the Irish Church being closely linked to the Vatican; MacMurrough defeated in 1166 – finally going out of the country to seek help from Henry II; and then in 1541, many Gaelic chieftains anglicising their titles and names, and finally Henry VIII King of Ireland and Head of the Church. And here I am writing about the need during troubled centuries for an individual in Ireland to appear sympathetic to Englishness, with a possible belief in Protestantism (belonging to any branch of the Western Church outside the Roman communion) suggesting to the civil authorities that they should be considered to be a person who is 'less of a threat'.

These leanings were generally to those of the educated middle class, whilst the poor lower classes held on to the Catholic Church for security. Language allows communication, and the form the language takes informs the few, or the many. Education – teaching proven facts, the result of scientific testing – remains the correct curriculum to take. People's responsibility through ownership gives interest, commitment and care. In times of hardship, bad harvests, having to pay back loans then to borrow yet again, lack of food, too few jobs, little or no representation, no education nor training (National Schools began 1831). These hardships do and did cause unrest and great unhappiness. This in turn makes those who are not so affected feel justifiably anxious, fearing that what they have will be taken away, by the many who existed without. It would be right to say that the whole population was in uproar.

This state of affairs affects all nations; it is how the poor are helped that makes for a settled society. Hope is a necessity for all people, and a liberally educated society the aim. A peaceful society relies upon a reasonable distribution of resources, enough available for tomorrow's workers; this increases prosperity and improves social advances. In Ireland the governing body lacked the support to deliver progress.

Family names in ancient times were derived from the Gaelic, in this instance 'ciar' (Ciardha) and Norman (French). English names or family names were adopted during the 17th and 18th centuries, when Irish names and family gatherings (Irish roots) were discouraged. During the 18th and 19th centuries, when the Irish language almost died away, the 'O' and 'Mac' were dropped from use. Later, these prefixes were restored when pride of Irishness became restored as 'no longer a threat'.

In the 18th and 19th centuries outlying areas of Ireland's countryside catered for small tenant farmers and farm labourers. Many others found work as servants, there being a large servant class. Throughout the ages the middle classes of Ireland tended to gravitate toward Ireland's main cities and to England, leaving their homes, farms and land in the hands of estate and land agents. They in turn split the land into smaller holdings to cater for the many who were poor, allowing for a safer spread of payments. When the owner or renter died sons and daughters took over, paying the rent and tithe, and perhaps splitting the land into yet smaller plots.

English estates are generally passed onto the eldest son, who may be the parents' attorney. His main task is to look after the growth and security of the holding to part divide when the children are old enough to benefit. In Ireland family estates are divided equally, giving each member of the family equal shares to do what they believe is appropriate for their needs. A comparison between the two forms of inheritance distinctly gives a reason why English estates tendered to remain large and perhaps complete. Castles, manor houses, moated farms, working farms, grand houses and parks are considered strategic, social, and economic holdings whilst whole. In Ireland land plots became smaller and smaller, and eventually became valueless. This continued until the plots of land could no longer sufficiently feed the family members, who would eventually have to leave to find better conditions elsewhere, helping those left to pay the rents and tithes by selling excess produce.

This tenant rent system is understandable from an ownership point of view, however it does need payments to be made and kept up to maintain the cycle. When that fails, which it did because the land became bare and unproductive, and the potato blight occurred later to finally obliterate any sort of food, starvation for the many was the result. Owners of the land, or agents of the rentable plots, have to, as far as possible, ensure that the offered plot maintains value/workability under all or most conditions. It comes down eventually to the humanity and responsibility of the owner. In many instances in the 17th and later centuries the owners of the land had little or no connection, relationship or association, with the society, place or country; they did not consider where they lived as home to be a place of security.

The ancient family groupings, which were led by a chief, lord or king, maintained their standing and position by assertion, proving themselves by acts of aggressive force, exhibiting power. This need to show leadership was, as it were, 'in the blood', even to the extent that they would suppress their own kith and kin. This aggression masked a deeper, closer look at where it was all leading – the shape of the future. The governing power was but temporally held; this allowed domination to enter surreptitiously, until all about had change. The new power was stronger and held on, to allow social understandings to be remoulded, to legislate a central government system as something fairer for all classes.

This story covers the King William IV reign 1765-1837, the start of Queen Victoria's reign 1837-1901, the Great Hunger of 1845, the Great Exhibition 1851, and the Crimean War 1854-6. It tells the story of an emigrant Irishman from Dublin in 1813 who dreamt of a new beginning. It traces the authenticity of his name, gives us some insight into his family history, touches on his forebears, his trade, home, marriage, children, and his introduction to London's society.

The story is told in three parts: (1) Thomas emigrates from Ireland to London; (2) Ester leaves home to become a seamstress; (3) The couple meet and get married. Each part is set in the early 1800s. The tale explains why they leave home, their journey, describes London's city life, how they both build a career, find love, plan a home, and begin a family. This is the start of a Kearey presence in London.

Thomas follows a dream, visualized over many years, as he completed his apprenticeship and survived his first few years as a journeyman. His dreams do not weaken but keep him steady – especially during the troubles in Ireland.

What is compelling is his fortitude; his long-term goals do come true. He is lucky to have the stamina and the will to succeed, which serves him well. He intends to become a Londoner, to get married, have a family and to give his children a safe and secure upbringing. These are common enough desires for any young man in England, but in 1800s Ireland they are almost fantasies – outlandish expectations.

This romantic adventure turns out to be a happy one. It is set in a period of relative prosperity when industry blossomed and paid wages, and jobs were available. Grattan's parliament was doing well. However, on the land things were not so prosperous. Land ownership was the problem, then and later.

Unfortunately the individual needed land to qualify to vote and the majority of the Catholic poor were without ownership, so they lost their voice. Meanwhile the Irish government had independence but not executive power; that was still in the hands of the Parliament in London, which brings us nicely back to our story. It is a true story where the main characters are real people, a story to pull the heartstrings and make you cry; it is intimate and revealing, a book not to be put down and certainly never forgotten. It is through Thomas and Ester that I too can live my dreams of building a greater love of family, and of the past.

Dublin Castle 1816. Today it is the Assay Office for gold and silver.

Thomas's story

A SUMMARY

Thomas Kearey (1791-1860) of Dublin moved to London and found a job, remaining at the same firm all his life. He had been trained as a smelter of metals, and his daily job was to collect the ore or unwanted metal which had been delivered, cut it up or crush it (to make its bulk smaller), prepare the pit with its cast-iron bowl, arrange the wood and charcoal, and perhaps some coal, which when lit burned off the wood, leaving both charcoal and coke to be tamped down to form the base at the bottom of the bowl, where holes drilled into the base allowed air to be forced in. Bricks surrounded the dish in the pit to help retain heat. Bellows forced in air to raise the temperature, which melted the ore and separated the metals. A tapping channel released slag and waste, allowing its molten parts to drain into a casting dish. Control of the heat was essential. Like all skills, experience helped, enabling the pure metal to be made to flow.

In 1813, boarding the package boat to Liverpool, Thomas made his way to the Golden Cross Inn, Charing Cross. It was generally known, even at the time, when Soho was referred to as 'Little Ireland', as the goal of the bulk of Irish immigrants. Questioning pawnbrokers about him as to where gold was refined, Thomas learned of Thomas Sirrell's business in Aldersgate, an area of London specialising in jewellery, precious metals and gold products. Making his way there he introduced himself to the owner, outlining his skills and presenting his trade certificate and introductory letter. His bearing and forthright approach impressed Mr Sirrell, who immediately gave him a job – to start the following day.

His next task was to find permanent lodgings within walking distance of his place of work. He ended up two miles away at Mrs Josie Whitehouse's guest house in Drury Lane, a half-hour walk. Thomas made himself the perfect guest and was welcomed by Josie, who housed him on the top floor. Over a period of time Thomas became a much-liked and respected guest, welcomed as 'dear friend', whilst continuing to work in the gold quarter of central London, close to Goldsmiths Hall.

Thomas worked for Sirrell's for almost two years, making a great impression. He took over the smelting side of the business and on many occasions took charge whilst Mr Sirrell was out buying in stock. Eventually Thomas Sirrell retired, and his business and building were taken over by William Bryer of W. Bryer & Sons, who operated a similar business next door. Thomas was retained, and advanced to become manager of the business.

On a visit one day to Mrs Rose Springer's dress and suit shop in Queensgate, off the Brompton Road, needing a shortening of the sleeves of a new jacket specially bought for the firm's annual dinner, he met Ester Pepler, who served him. Thomas was infatuated by her charm and loveliness, and looked forward to renewing their acquaintance the following week when picking up his jacket. He was not disappointed; his longings were heightened. Thomas wanted to get to know Ester better and perhaps take her out for a walk. He invited her to his lodgings, to a dinner party especially laid on by Josie in Ester's honour. Thomas fetched her by coach and introduced her to Josie and her friend Steven James, the fourth member of the party. Steven was the stage manager of the Globe Theatre and a wonderful raconteur.

The party was a great success, and led to Thomas and Ester becoming engaged to be married. Josie offers them her top floor whilst they collect for their bottom drawer. They meanwhile cleaned and decorated, furnished and hung curtains to make their apartment perfect for their stay. Josie had specified that she was shortly to retire, hoping that Ester would make the business prosper for as long as possible, a period, of at least two years.

Thomas and Ester planned excitedly to make the top floor their haven. The couple agreed that they should not engage in intercourse during their engagement for fear of pregnancy. Gradually they became more intimate and frank, preparing their own perfect home together and telling each other their innermost thoughts and fears and how they would bring up and educate their children.

In 1819 their friends and workmates attended the couple's marriage at St. Anne's Church, Soho, and their subsequent wedding breakfast. It was hailed by all attending as the betrothal of two of the kindest people ever. The following year, a son, also Thomas, was born, continuing an ancient family custom.

The principal figures in the story

1. Thomas Kearey b1791, Dublin. Apprenticed gold and silver smelter and refinery 1804-11, Dublin Assay Office, Goldsmiths of the Guild of all Saints which existed in the 15th century incorporated by Royal Charter by Charles I. Re-incorporated 1637, to include clock and watchmakers. Father, John Kearey b1770, mother Elizabeth (Osbourne), brother, Henry and sister's Elizabeth, Charlotte, and Eleanor. Thomas immigrated to London 1814.
2. Ester Pepler b1794, of Great Stanmore. Left school at 14 in 1808. Trainee dress maker to Mrs Rose Springer (Rosie) of The Milliners, Old Brompton Road. Remained with her for 11 years, becoming fully trained, capable of running the shop.
3. Thomas Sirrell 1815, chronometer and jewellery shop. 53-54, Aldersgate, at the tail end of St. Martin's Le Grand, a small road between the Post Office

and St. Martin's Church, Aldersgate Street. Thomas Sirrell's chronometer shop, also gold and silver refiner and smelter of wholesale and retail gold and silver, jewellers, watchmakers, diamond jewellery and plate valued, bought, and sold, bookbinders, dentists, and photographers. Waste refined and purchased. It was at this shop that Thomas Kearey received his specialist training.

4. W. Bryer & Sons, gold refiners, of 55, Aldersgate Street, Barbican, next door to Thomas Sirrell. W. Bryer & Sons bought out numbers 53-54 in 1820, absorbing the business, when Thomas Sirrell died. Thomas stayed with the firm throughout his life, becoming the firm's manager.
5. Steven James – Stage Manager of the Opera House, Mary Street.
6. Mrs. Rose Springer (in her late sixties) of Springer's milliners and gowns, suits and shoes of 12, Queen Gate Place, off Queensgate, Old Brompton Road and Cromwell Road. Trained Ester Pepler as a dress maker. Ester was with her for 11 years, until she was 25.
7. Mrs Josie Whitehouse (in her late sixties) proprietor of a guest house in 56, Drury Lane, between Long Acre Church and Russell Street. Housed Thomas Kearey for 4 year.
8. Mr William (Bill) Turner, resident jewellery designer at W. Bryer & Sons.

9. Daniel Larking of Thurloe Square, South Kensington (opposite South Kensington Museum). Master builder, painter and stainer. Engaged to refurbish the couple's top floor.

10. Thomas Tennant, household furniture maker. Warehouse in Long Lane, Soho. Westminster.

PART 1

CHAPTER 1

Planning a future in England

Thomas Kearey had planned his migration for some time, looked forward to it, dreamt of it, prayed for it. The journey, finding a job and lodgings, sampling life in London, anything more than that, were distractions. These he kept to the back of his mind, as he had needed every ounce of strength to get this far.

This tale invites you to accompany Thomas as he makes his way to London and seeks work and lodgings, and to learn of his life afterwards. First and foremost, he had no intention of turning tail, whatever trials and tribulations he was to meet along the way; he intended to be there for the rest of his life and make a success of it come what may. He did not intend to end up in the alehouse.

His long-distance planning included marriage, having children and finally retiring, having made a success of his efforts. There was no thought of ever returning to Ireland. He had seen the life of Dublin around him as an indentured apprentice, and knew the bulk of Irish people were tenant farmers who sold excess produce to pay their rent; their daily lives did not include planning for bad winters, failed crops or cruel debt collectors. Survival to see the week out was far more important.

Families were usually large by today's standards. There was no contraception, only withdrawal or abstinence, and very little sexual information, only word of mouth. What formal education there was was closely linked with religious teaching, dictated by convention, certainly not scientce. Children worked the land as soon as they could and were shown what to do and how to do it, even if it was only to scatter seed for the chickens and pour swill for the pigs. It was unusual for the elder boys not to eventually copy their fathers and keep whatever business, trade, shop or farm they ran afloat to pass on to the next generation.

It was the alehouse that played the major part in an Irishman's home life. Here he learnt the news of the day and enjoyed the company of his companions, and in the winter its fire was his only warmth. If he belonged to a club, then the great room upstairs was the scene of an annual dinner. As a rule the beerhouse was the only place for amusement and company. His life was reduced to the most crude and simple form. In 1790 it was unlikely that the majority could read or write, and those that could did so imperfectly. Language used was that of the area, not uniform to the country's own. If today that sounds weird or unusual, it was not. Until universal education was introduced, a standard curriculum was adhered to and an individual's rights were not even given space, let alone considered.

When Thomas was born at the latter end of the 17th century, Protestant England was faced by a Catholic coalition of France, Austria and Spain, and America was seeking independence. France and Spain declared war on Britain, taking the American side. Great Britain was under continuous threat. The English army in America retired, unsure how to react when facing the American Army's guerrilla tactics – their fast-moving opportunistic strikes used familiar muskets and long-learned hunting skills which stood them in good stead.

Thomas had been brought up strictly by his parents into the Protestant religion in Dublin, attending the church along with his parents. He attended the church school and services throughout his life. At no stage did he question his faith or his church, its strictures and its power, nor blame the church for the country's parlous state. He blamed the greed of the country's aristocracy and moneyed middle-class.

The Irish Protestants of Ireland dusted down their weapons and checked their flints and powder, intending to volunteer, ready to defend their country. Britain's military leader in America, General Cornwallis, and his men marched out and surrendered at Yorktown; this unsteadied the British Government, giving the Irish Catholics hope that they would receive better treatment. The Irish smallholders had just started to hear news of the latest farming developments in England, which involved using soil improvement techniques and advanced animal husbandry to increase both yield and profitability. They appreciated change was needed, but why should they improve the soil for the land's owners, who were never there? Nor did the majority care or even understand.

Was this a good time for this tall, handsome young Irishman, not long out of his time as an apprentice, to strike out and take a gamble on finding true love and happiness? There was no way anybody was going to stop him; he was fired up, raring to go, to follow his dreams. He had the backing of his parents and friends. Others had done this, so why shouldn't he?

Having finished his seven-year apprenticeship in 1811, he had continued working at the coach and harness makers for two years to gain vital knowledge. Now he had his ticket booked, ready to attend the boarding procedure at the Dublin quayside and to march up the gang-plank and catch the packet boat to Liverpool. He thought he looked English, having dressed in clothes he believed would match an Englishman's. He also tried to assume English behaviour and manner, but was that going to be enough? This was not because he hated all things Irish but because he intended his new life to have all the security and lasting happiness that London could offer. He had to integrate and fit in.

Ireland was caught up not just in a religious dispute but a longing throughout all the middle-classes for nationhood. Thomas' limited experience, gained listening to family discussions, gave him sufficient insight to appreciate that none of what he was planning was going to be easy. He had seen for himself how those who were less well educated and trained had to fight to make their lives secure. Adapting to English ways in all things would support him and make his life easier.

Back home in the countryside, the major land areas were divided up into small lots of one or two acres and rented out. The harvests had to be sold to cover buying in new seed potatoes and other vegetables, plus saving the following year's rent. Good harvests would just about see these tenant farmers through. Poor harvests, on the other hand, would mean starvation, misery and even eviction. The potato blight began in the Americas; how long would it take to turn up in Ireland?

The fertile grasslands of Ireland were split into smaller and smaller areas. Inheritance further divided what was left. The population the land had to provide for increased, and eventually varied crop production rested solely on a versatile potato diet. When that failed, because of poor land management and lack of plant knowledge, people went hungry. On top of this poorly-managed public health issue, a potato disease threatened what was already an imminent disaster.

The fungus that caused the potato to rot, *Phytophthora infestans*, survives and propagates, contained in its spore container. These containers, when mature, become detached by wind and rain. In the damp, moist, warm air, the spores, called zoospores, swim away and settle. The fermentation and decay of the potato leaf gives nourishment, while the protoplasm stimulates the fungus. More rain washes the blight down into the soil, contaminates it, enters the potato and depending on weather and collection conditions, remains there to become the following year's seed potato. To prevent blight reinfection, you have to spray during summer before late summer rains. Ireland's potato crisis – evictions, fever and starvation – was all part of the great famine.

When Thomas died in 1820, he left behind a society that was still locked up in an ancient tithe and land division system which was born of the Middle Ages; out of date, unfair and certain to eventually lead to disaster, which it did. He could see, during his last few years as a journeyman, how life for the unfortunate many was likely to be if their harvest failed. His parents and relations spoke of the horrors too many times not to have a lasting effect upon his mind. He 'wanted out' and intended to start afresh elsewhere.

The upper classes wanted all the country to be converted to Protestantism – it was to their advantage – but they were still ordered to pay tithes to the Catholic Church and not work in crown offices, and to this they naturally objected. Their property rights were never held back though, nor stopped; they were still able to own a weapon, vote, and sit in Parliament. This meant that in times when self-rule was the cry they could be never be relied upon to defend the country's English connection.

The Catholics teetered on the brink of 'getting their own back', even if it meant wiping out every bossy Protestant. In the end, about the time between when Thomas was born till he walked up the gang-plank, there emerged in Ireland a struggle for the poor majority to assume political power, as they had been having to bear increasingly high rents and suffer lack of security; the vote would have shown how desperate the situation was. Thomas was impatient and was not prepared to suffer all the setbacks. He had the strength, knowledge, and skills of a young man in his prime wanting all that life could afford now, and did not want to wait for a damaged society to sort itself out.

Before we carry the tale forward I should step back for a moment and explain about Ireland's historic metal mining, which has been traced back to the Bronze Age. Iron, copper, alum, lead and silver were mined through the centuries. By the 1700s the iron industry was much reduced, due to land clearance cutting down trees used as fuel. The industry took off once more, stimulated by Britain's industrial revolution. In the next century there was a gold rush in Co. Wicklow which passed from individuals to State intervention 1796-1803 and then back again to individuals 1804-39, and privately in 1860. The Irish mining depression carried on through to later times. When Thomas was apprenticed as a gold and silver smelter during the early gold rush period, which passed on his knowledge and skills needed by the industry in London.

Carved monument saved from London's blitz depicting the smelter's job.

CHAPTER 2

Taking ship

The fresh salt air blew away Thomas' doubts and fears as he strolled around the deck thrusting back his shoulders and taking deep breaths. He was going to show them, although he wasn't quite sure who 'they' were. His trade skills, he thought, would stand him in good stead. Although he had stayed in Dublin after his apprenticeship to extend his knowledge, he had never been outside the city boundary, so this adventure was an enormous gamble and not something he undertook likely.

Thomas stood before the mast looking out over the rail as Ireland grew smaller. The grassy headland of his homeland was now almost lost. He prayed that his parents, brother and sisters would be all right. The mass of people were in a dangerous mood, and it was highly likely that the hotheads would cause unrest and fear.

Dublin had at one time been the capital of the northern Celtic Nation, and it was the British Isles' second largest capital city, with many graceful mansions and public buildings. The city's finest days were in the 18th century, although the population continued to rise without enough housing to accommodate the numbers which were to create enormous slums. As with the plight of the land, not enough care was taken to maintain its one-time grand position

There are some indelible parts to Thomas' past life. His name was given by an important family birthright to all first-born sons. His given name of Thomas was to remind him that Christ and Christianity would give him daily support and everlasting life and that was drummed into his consciousness. It was the name once given to 'Doubting Thomas', who would not believe Christ had risen from the dead and sought proof by thrusting his hand into Christ's side where the Roman's javelin had penetrated. Thereafter, Doubting Thomas became a dedicated disciple, and later a venerated saint.

Our strolling disciple with the same name, having had it drummed into him along with his religious beliefs, descended to the next deck below, found a seat and put down his bag. Looking about, he noticed some of the other passengers. A number of families were grouped together, some obviously-working class men looking bewildered and unsure and also seeking work. There were two women, one pregnant, the other, a friend, fussing over her.

The ship gave a lurch and rolled to one side; they had left the landing stage and sailed into midstream, heading east towards the river's mouth and the Irish Sea beyond, with sails set for the westerly blowing them to Liverpool Docks.

Below deck saloon

Thomas was leaving behind his father John and mother Elizabeth, née Osborne, his brother, Henry, and his sisters, Elizabeth, Charlotte, and Eleanor, all those he loved and cherished. This spurred him on to make a success of his sacrifice. He heard tales of others who had done the same thing, except that they had reached out to English-speaking countries further afield. He had thought this through. His skills as a gold and silver refiner and smelter, plus his experience working with more commercial casting metals, gave him the versatility needed in London, with its vast population, where he had heard they were starting to dig out a new canal system.

The family waved him goodbye

He had had the family's blessing before leaving, receiving their full support and love. Now he had to do what he had promised – to make a success of his move. His Gaelic given-name in Irish was Tomaltach, derived from Tomailt, meaning provisions, good living or plentiful food and used to signify a man of hospitality; the name is also derived from the Irish, as tomhas, which is a measure, and from Tomhas – by metathesis (the transportation of sounds into words) and the proper noun for Thomas.

He was pleased that a relation, an ancestor of Keary of Fore, County Westmeath, believed to be a branch of the

Cahill family of Connaught, suggested to his relations that they should become more closely associated with the English national religion and nation, assuming the name and spelling of Keary with a K and an ey and abandon the prefix O' and the Carey or Cary form of spelling. He knew that O'Ciardha (an ancient Irish Surname) had been mentioned by the Four Masters in the tenth century as chiefs of Cairbre O'Ciardha, now the barony of Carbery, once the Hy-Niall Septs of Ulster, Meath and Connaught. This had been accepted and adopted by his relations and passed down him.

Liverpool harbour and docks, 1800

Thomas felt at ease when asked for his name to be entered onto the ship's manifest before he boarded ship in Dublin docks. He was going to have enough problems finding lodgings and a job without having to face negative responses from every facet of London's society. From here on he was to assume Englishness.

CHAPTER 3

The adventure begins

Thomas boarded ship in Dublin with his carpet-bag of tools clenched in his hand. His proven skill as a gold refiner and smelter was going to have to stand him in good stead. He had every right to believe that having a knowledge of metallurgy, the science as applied to the production of metal alloys, and the engineering of metal components used in products for both consumers and manufacturers, was needed in London's industries.

Thomas left Ireland knowledgeable about smelting and refining metals, and it was to this trade that he was to turn to seek a new start in life and full-time employment to fulfil his promise to his family back home in Dublin, something he did not intend to renege on.

The golden age of canals in London was between 1770 and 1830. At that time the mail and fire engine were hauled by wagon and coach, public service transport for pedestrians by horse-drawn bus. There were no individual mains water or gas services to homes and only a rather primitive waste-water sewer. Hay, wood, coal and stone were delivered by barge alongside the Thames embankment.

The smelting and hammering of iron was necessary for the construction of cart and carriage tyres, axles needed moulding and brackets and angle-irons required drilling. During his apprenticeship he had learned all these skills to gain his certificate. He intended to apply for a job in the precious metal industry which he heard so much about.

On the coach journey down from the Liverpool docks to London's coach station at Charing Cross, Thomas was comparing the countryside to that of his home country. There was certainly greater activity by the populations of villages and towns, and everything appeared bigger and more regimented. Fields were larger and hedged, stone walls ran along most sides of the road, surfaces were laid with a camber, kerbs were laid in and drainage ditches and grips dug, to take away surface water. It was a revelation which he never forgot.

Back home the poor tenant farmers, who were mainly Catholic, only farmed one or two acres. As he travelled along, Thomas could see that the fields were larger, as were the farms. It gave home a negative backward image, for there the production of food was unable to cope with what was demanded from it.

Thomas felt sad as he tried to rationalise his thoughts. Thankfully, what was about him as the coach travelled along kept his mind too busy for sadness. The journey had frequent stops to change horses and perhaps one overnight stay at an inn.

His excitement was immense and his trepidation infectious. He was in his best clothes, including a hat purposely bought for the occasion. If he kept quiet he could be mistaken for an Englishman. He nervously checked his buttons and adjusted his cravat, and noticed his hands were trembling. He jerked himself upright. This was no good. He was here to stay and make a success of life, and he had to get on with it.

Taking a seat on the outside with ten others, his journey carried him through Warrington and eighteen other towns to arrive at the Gold Cross Inn, Charing-Cross, taking seven hours, stopping to change horses every ten to fifteen miles.

It was a journey that convinced him that he was right to believe England was the place to be to make one's fortune, given half a chance. He was envious of what he had already seen; this is what he was wanting, and he was eager to experience it.

It was later that the Metropolitan Board of Works was given power to design a drainage system. Bazalgette's plan was for a sewerage system which drained from Hackney to Stamford Hill, Chiswick to Crystal Palace, transferring London's sewage to outfalls well outside human habitation. Later the London County Council (LCC) took over the administration of London. These improvements were to come about at the time when Thomas was approaching London, and life for Londoners was dangerous, thanks to diseases such as cholera, which was to cause a great number of deaths. The new waste water sewers were not to come about for another lifetime.

The coach made its way into the London suburbs from St Albans down the Great North Road, passing Barnet and Stanmore along the Edgware Road. The Charing Cross drop-off for the passengers, outside the Golden Cross Inn, was close to Trafalgar Square, the Embankment keeping back the River Thames at high tide, and the Savoy Theatre

Thomas would see for himself how cosmopolitan London was. It was the largest city in the world, with its own docks, and he felt there had to be a place for him.

London was the ruling classes' playground and had a

Golden Cross coaching inn, 1820

blend of formality and the picturesque, one-time royal parks and gardens, observatories and ship builders, military establishments and museums. Kensington Gardens was open to the public on one day each week. Hyde Park was on its eastern side. Both had all that visitors and picnickers would want. Running was banned, as were rowdy games. Coaches ran in all weathers and conditions.

At last the coach pulled up outside the Golden Inn at Charing Cross. This was the terminus, where horses stabled and drivers picked up the next coach for the return journey. If you listened hard you would hear the coach horn as the post coach came in from the south.

Jumping down, Thomas reached for his bag, and with a cheery farewell he marched on his way up the road to Soho, to Frith Street and Dean Street. There must be lodgings there; this was the heart of Soho, in Westminster. He was aware that he should make for Soho, because there were many Irish expatriates there who might give him board and lodging until he could find a job. Having asked the way from the coachman, he made his way through the crowded streets carrying his tools. Keeping his shoes out of the filthy pools of water and piles of horse droppings was no easy matter as he marched up St Martins Lane.

He asked at a likely boarding house for a room; he couldn't wait to put down his bag and get some sleep. Fortunately the landlady was sympathetic and kind, allowing him to take a room. Now he could relax and work out how he was going to find a job. The next day was going to point the way to success or failure. He was asleep as soon as his head touched the pillow.

The following morning the guest house was alive with shouts and the bustle of maids, and cooks, deliveries and early starters preparing for their day. Outside, the streets were filled with street vendors and cleaners collecting up the horse droppings before the mass of citizens started work. Cows were kept inside and outside the city, and other animals too, those bound for the table, were also afforded a home as were pet animals, hounds and horses. It takes very little imagination to picture the sounds, smells and effects of an abundance of people closely living and working together. It was an organised chaos of city dwellers intent upon claiming their place before anyone else. He took in the streets, alleyways, doorways, steps, cellars and cobbles, the filled horse troughs, railings, and shop displays, coaches, omnibuses, Hansom cabs, dog carts and barrows; he saw all the delivery men, crossing-sweepers, costermongers, porters, clerks, soldiers, office workers, milliners, priests and nuns, tobacconists, tea shops. inns and policemen, servants, beggars, thieves and embezzlers, flower girls, sellers of fire logs, kindling and coal, candle-makers, street entertainers and pickpockets. The roads were bursting with life, and the stench was indescribable. The printers were using hand-set metal type, lithographic artists drew on stone, and their handbills peppered the walls and sandwich boards blocked the paths. There were newspaper sellers, poster displays and advertisements, darting delivery boys, chamber pots being emptied, night-soil men just finishing, to off-load to fertilize adjacent farms. Vegetable peelings and slurry lay underfoot. On the embankment just a stone's throw away were square riggers, barques, barges, cutters, tugs, skiffs, row-boats and the homeless, all using the River Thames as a highway, lavatory or waste disposal facility.

CHAPTER 4

Finding a job

Thomas had to share a room with three others, but he slept well. He made sure that he had a wash at the pump outside and that his clothes were respectable. He knew his first task was to find a job. After having something to eat and drink, he walked around Soho looking in the shops and workplaces. There were any number of pawnbrokers all vying with each other. Thomas knew there had to be a gold refiner who bought up gold to melt down for watches and jewellery.

Thomas had served his seven-year apprenticeship by 1811, working as a journeyman for two more years to perfect his skills, and here he was now as a skilled journeyman at the age of twenty-three with a good understanding of the smelting, refining and casting of most metals. He made it his business to acquaint himself with melting points of all metals.

Extracting the melted ore ready to pour into moulds.

At last he found somebody who knew an assayers, W. Bryer & Sons, Gold Refiners, Aldersgate Street and Barbican. This was to be his first call with his journeyman's certificate. He started walking along the Embankment towards St Pauls, having been told that behind St Pauls were St Martins Church and the Post Office, all very near to Goldsmith's Hall at the bottom of Aldersgate Street.

He set out with a bounce in his step, carrying his bag of tools and being careful not to leave them behind in case they were stolen. He had a stroke of luck with the last pawnbroker, as the man had a connection with Ireland.

It was just after midday when Thomas reached the Barbican and noticed Thomas Sirrell's premises, founded five years before in 1815, according to the engraved plaque outside the door. Whilst he was there he thought he might as well go in and introduce himself. He stepped through the front door of number 54 determined to present a good impression.

"Good morning sir, my name is Thomas Kearey," he said, thrusting out his hand. Mr Sirrell shook it and told him to put his bag down. When they both introduced themselves as Thomas, it brought laughter, which reduced the tension and lightened the younger man's embarrassment.

Thomas presented his signed and completed indenture papers and explained his knowledge and interests, telling Thomas Sirrell that much of his gold experience had been casting buckles, buttons and walking stick handle rings, and that he had moved from Ireland to gain more experience.

It was a fortunate meeting. Thomas Sirrell needed another worker to allow him to concentrate on his jewellery, his first love, and he took a fancy to this upright Irishman who seemed so pleasant and relaxed. They agreed that Thomas should start the following day, after agreeing a starting wage that would increase after three months. They shook hands, the door was opened and out into the fresh air walked Thomas, hardly believing his good fortune.

Later Thomas found that Thomas Sirrell and the business next door, recognising that they were using the same metals and devices, often helped each other out. The house next door, number 53, was owned by John Bryer & Sons, a watch and clock maker which later specialised in jewellery and gold plate smelted down to re-cast. In 1894, Thomas Sirrell retired, the businesses merged in 1900, both buildings were pulled down and rebuilt. W. Bryer & Sons continues in business in Hatton Garden to this day.

Thomas walked back to Soho slowly drawing in deep breaths, afraid that something dreadful must happen. Now that he knew what he could afford, he had to find permanent lodgings. He had already been told that rooms were available in west London, an area which was about to undergo many changes as the London canals were being dug out. It was nearly midday as he made his way back to Soho.

The designing of canals started in 1800; they were purpose-built to carry heavy produce: coal, timber, bricks, potatoes, and sand, cement, gravel and stone. There was no competition at first; the canal building continued until the railways took over. Initially the cartage of building material covered the development of West London with its houses, flats, roads and bridges. Labour was needed to load and offload barges, build and decorate the new building works and go on to attend to the infrastructure. When the first tracks were laid in about 1810, the transport of goods by horse and barge stopped almost immediately. Robert Stephenson's Rocket (1812) convinced the investors that rail was the answer to the mass transportation of goods. It was another 13 years before it took its first passengers in 1825.

It was clear that Thomas' plan and execution were

opportune for the future Kearey family. There was never any cause for worry about an occupation during this and later periods. A major development of north-west London started in the 1800s. The existing tenants were turned out of their homes, which were then flattened and new buildings erected. The Peabody Buildings, blocks of flats, gave shelter for many. The land was cleared, roads laid, and bricklaying began.

Canals, houses, and railway lines were constructed in that order, with the infrastructure to go with them; schools, churches, stations and shops were to follow later. Thomas had chosen his emigration time perfectly. Over the next fifty years he would be converted from provincial Irishman to Londoner.

There were poor and homeless, immigrants, sick children, and the elderly, beggars and the displaced. The building firms employed mostly Irish labour. Later the Metropolitan Railway Company destroyed 1,000 houses to make way for a new railway station for Paddington. The homeless travelled from one empty building to another before they were knocked down. There was no sanitation, and the stench was unbearable. The public baths charged according to the temperature of the water; a cold second-class bath was a penny. Soup kitchens abounded. A night's lodging cost 2d or 3d with the use of a pail. Workhouses were full, as were the arches under bridges. At night the homeless sought shelter in every nook and cranny.

Thomas walked along, determined to find permanent

lodgings. As he got nearer to The Strand, he turned right just past the Globe Theatre and walked up Drury Lane towards Longacre, passing Russell Street on the left then, almost up to the church, he came to number 56 Drury Lane, and saw a notice for a vacancy. It turned out to be a room on the upper floor for 40d a night or £2 a week all found, including the use of a wash room. The proprietor, a Mrs Josie Whitehouse, had obviously been a theatre performer. She noticed Thomas' bag and inquired what was in it. This allowed Thomas to bring up his new job as a gold and precious metal refiner.

The woman had been a dancer and singer, and was au fait with the world of entertainment and its drawbacks and delights. Drury Lane society was her world now, and as the owner of a boarding house her clientele kept her alive to the latest top performers and shows. She had never met anyone quite like Thomas. He was a confident twenty-three year old who had secured a job on his first day in a strange city.

Her mothering instincts got the better of her. "Now you come along with me and I'll show you around your new home. Here is the guests' sitting room – I only allow my guests to sit in here in the evening. The breakfast room also leads off the hallway, where guests come in the morning between the hours of seven to nine. I don't serve a lunch and the dinner is served at seven. The lumber room is where you keep your luggage, cases and trunks etc. The room is kept locked so there's no need to worry about losing anything. Only I can open it and lock it."

She kept up a continuous chatter about everything, while Thomas, fascinated, replied with the occasional exclamation of wonder, hoping he was showing enough polite interest. She continued, "My daily helps arrive at six and leave at eight. The kitchens and laundry room are at the end of the hall. My girls attend to everything and they're answerable to me if there's any hanky-panky." She hesitated here, stopped and looked at Thomas. "You do understand what I mean, I suppose." Thomas nodded his head with a smile. There was no way he was going to spoil this lucky break. "Certainly, madam."

She was surprised at how sure she felt about Thomas' answer, and was now even more flummoxed by her feelings. "Good," she said, "Now I must get on. I'll see you and the other guests later." With that she went down the hall to the kitchen. She noticed she was a little unsteady on her feet. What on earth was the matter with her? She well understood the effect Thomas had had upon her!

To regain some semblance of calmness, Thomas went off to find something to eat and drink. He walked up Aldersgate Road, making sure he knew how to get back. Thinking over the morning's events, he felt relief that he had acted with politeness and consideration to both Mr Sirrell and Mrs Whitehouse. He had not expected to have found a job quite so easily, and knowing that he was to start work the next day was astonishing. He could not believe his luck.

Aldersgate Street, close to the gold quarter of London.

CHAPTER 5

Aldersgate Street

Now Thomas had a room booked for the next month. He had much to write about to his parents; he could picture them sitting round the fire as his father read out his letter.

Passing an inn close to St Bartholomew's Hospital, he stopped and went into the bar, looking for a glass of ale and some bread and cheese. He found a corner opposite the bar, and sat there listening to what was going on around him as he tucked into his bread and cheese and tankard of ale, finding that he was hungrier than he had first thought. The bar was packed with workers, men who occupied their places most days, all talking at once mostly about their wives.

When he had finished his lunch, he decided to walk around the whole district to familiarise himself with what activities, businesses and people there were and imagine how he was going to fit in and become a resident. He still couldn't get over the fact that he was going to start work the next morning and was looking forward to the experience. Already he had noticed how different the people and the street society were from home. There was a greater mix of people, from city gentlemen to clerks, from post office workers to laundry maids and from chimney sweeps to road sweepers.

The afternoon went by quickly. He was pleased he had decided to familiarise himself with the neighbourhood he was going to be living in with its numerous doorways, cobblestone alleys, and railings guarding basements below pavement level. Horses abounded: carriage horses, cabs, delivery carts, dog carts and the occasional hearse.

He arrived back to the boarding house two hours later at five o'clock to write to his parents, get comfortable in his bedroom and take his clothes out of the carpet bag to hang them up. In he went, feeling very unsure, bumping into another guest. They shook hands, introducing themselves. The middle-aged man was Steven James, who work round the corner at the Opera House as a stage manager. They joked about Thomas' work with gold. They both went up the stairs together and parted when Steven reached his on the second floor.

Thomas remembered about his bag being in the Locker Room and had to go back down. He knocked on the kitchen door to be answered by the cook. She shouted out for

Mrs Whitehouse, who came out of the sewing room. "Ah Thomas, I thought it might be you. Of course you can have your bag!" she said. They returned to the lobby, where the door was unlocked and the bag produced. "There we are. Is everything satisfactory?"

"Yes," replied Thomas, "I've had a lovely day." With that he ascended the stairs again to reach his room at the top.

As he sorted out his belongings, his mind was taken back to his people at home. They would be so surprised by where he had landed up, what he had done and where he had been. It seemed like a dream, achieving all that he had in so short a time.

After hanging and putting away his few clothes he settled down to write to his parents, telling them all the exciting news. Time flew by as he became lost in his writings.

At work, Thomas concentrated on satisfying Mr Bryer. He did his best to observe all the rules and habits of his staff, taking particular notice of the way moulds were made, the molten metal poured, and then the item smoothed and polished. He meant to be an ideal worker and learn as much as he could.

Making friends with all the staff wasn't easy, but over time they began to see how Thomas considered not only them and their interests but his own involvement with all that went on. He was always early arriving and late leaving, and took time to keep the workplace clean and tidy. They noticed how quickly he became one of them, using his undoubted skills with metal to suggest new ways of making the different lines Bryer's were offering.

Time went by quickly. On his days off, Thomas visited every museum and open house to gain as much knowledge as he could. He had won though and soon achieved his goal. W. Bryer & Sons made him manager of the furnace department, smelter and refinery, of both wholesale and retail sections of the business. It was what Thomas had worked towards, spending as much time as he could experiencing every aspect of the business. Talking to the staff was essential to understand what they were doing and how they fitted in with the rest of the business.

The next four years were spent in dedicated learning about the business. Mr Sirrell had retired not long after he had been first engaged, and later passed away. Thomas owed him a great deal; he had had faith in whatever Thomas did or said, relying upon him to turn out good work and to see that others did too.

The next door neighbour, John Bryer, had taken over Sirrell's company to enlarge his floor space, increase his staff and diversify the business. He combined his jewellery business with Sirrell's timepieces so that he could concentrate on jewellery and fashionable objects rather than chronometers. The smelting side consisted of dealing with bought in gold and silver to be melted down re-moulded or sold on.

The war with Napoleon's France had been won by the Duke of Wellington with the aid of the Prussians, and had been followed up by celebrations up and down the country. The Bryer business had done well out of the event, casting objects to celebrate the occasion, with rings and necklaces and engraved silver drinking goblets showing the duke's likeness. The American War of Independence came to an end at about at the same time, with a peace treaty. Thomas was now twenty-six. The two wars had drained the country's exchequer, but there was a relaxation on spending after the Treaty of Ghent had been signed.

Thomas was still living in Josie Whitehouse's home, but he had been moved down to the next floor and now had two rooms which were larger, two wardrobes and chest of drawers, with the wash room now on the same floor. He was happy there and had made a good friend of Josie, whose mothering instincts had been given full rein in looking after Thomas, who was in turn putting his efforts into making the guest house a meeting house for many of the businesses around. He had a small circle of friends, mostly from the jewellery business, and attended the occasional dance, or firm's dinner.

One of his friends had suggested dancing lessons and they both attended, meeting the same people each week. It was a new experience to have close contact with a woman, put his arm around her waist and hold her hand while looking into her face. He was embarrassed when his arm brushed his partner's breast. He never forgot his first dance, the music, the closeness of the ladies around him and the way they moved. He became an accomplished dancer, and his partners, impressed by his easy chatter and bonhomie, never refused a dance.

He never forgot his parents, his brother Henry and sisters; Elizabeth, Charlotte and Eleanor, keeping in touch by letter every month. He had a lot to be grateful for. Now was he going to open himself up to the possibility of marriage? He just had to talk to Josie. Perhaps there was a special church dispensation that he should abide by?

PART 2

CHAPTER 6

Ester

The Bryer business was staging its annual dinner and dance for the staff. As manager, Thomas had the task of organising the occasion, acting as Master of Ceremonies and ensuring the event was well attended. He had no option; he had to face up to it and do his best. He realised that he would have to buy a new suit, or certainly a new jacket. In the end he chose a jacket from a local shop. Unfortunately when he got home he found the sleeves didn't fit properly – they were too long. He must have them shortened. Thomas was advised by Josie Whitehouse to take the jacket to a shop in Queensgate, just off the Cromwell Road.

On his next Saturday afternoon off work, Thomas made his way past the Embankment down the Strand to Queens

Gate Place, where a Mrs Rose Springer had her dress and suit shop. It didn't take him long to get there and knock on the door. It was opened by a young woman, one of the staff, who invited him in to ask him how she could help. He was immediately struck by how lovely she was. Thomas told her about the sleeves, and she asked him to put the jacket on to see how much they needed shortening. He took the coat out of the bag he was carrying and placed it on the work bench, then took off his old everyday jacket and put the new one on, feeling very exposed as he did so, trying to look away, which he found very difficult to do because of her attractiveness.

He put his new jacket on and she busied herself smoothing it out, pulling down the sleeves and tucking up the excess, marking where she believed they should be shortened, to show off just the right amount of shirt cuff.

"There sir, is that how much cuff you would like to show?" she asked.

Thomas walked towards a long mirror, flexing his arm. "Yes, I believe that's just about right."

"Right then sir, I will mark just how much that is with this chalk." She kept looking at him, and he could not take his eyes off her. She carefully took the jacket off and laid it down on the work bench. Smoothing out the sleeves she measured out each, carefully making sure they were exactly the same length.

She smiled. "Now sir, I can have your jacket ready for next Saturday if that is convenient for you?" Thomas replied that that would be fine saying "Now, how much will that be?" Ester replied. "That will be just one shilling sir."

All the while Thomas was wondering how he could be sure he was making the right impression on her. He politely asked, "Could you tell me your name, just in case you are not here when I arrive?"

"I'm Ester, and I'm always here every Saturday afternoon. I'll make quite sure that I will not miss you then." She gave him a warm smile.

Thomas was never to forget his first meeting with Ester, how she looked and the way she behaved, the way she moved, the way she talked. He was completely captivated by her, right from the first.

He walked home along the Brompton Road to Hyde Park Corner. He was pleased to have the walk back along what he believed to be the most interesting streets in London. Now he could carefully take stock of what had happened. He had never before had such a shock to the system; he was hot, sweating, and breathing strongly, perhaps even shaking. The woman in the shop, what was her name? Was it Ester or Hester? It was Ester, he was quite sure. She was stunning, and he was determined to see her again. He found he was walking quickly, eager to get back to the guest house to tell Josie Whitehouse about her after dinner that night.

For the rest of the day Thomas kept on going over his meeting with Ester, what they had both said, what the shop had looked like inside, the way she filled the room with everything she did.

Finally it came to dinner time at the guest house. He descended the stairs, coming upon Josie at the bottom. He caught her off guard, and asked her if she minded giving her opinion about his future. Not knowing what he was talking about, she agreed to have a word with him after dinner. The last diner finished, and the table was cleared away and prepared for breakfast the next day. All was quiet when Josie came in and sat down. Thomas sat opposite and cleared his throat. He had thought through all that he was going to say umpteen times, but when it came to it he was tongue tied. She could see that he was having difficulty, so she stood up and asked if he would like a drink. To this he agreed, and she prepared two glasses of port. They settled down once more.

"Now what's this all about? I can see you are worried."

"No" said Thomas, "not worried, just uncertain". He went through his meeting with Ester, why he had been at the shop and its outcome, saying that he was to return the following week. He open up to Josie about being so pleasantly surprised by how easy and comfortable he had found it talking to Ester, and that he found her so lovely, something he had not felt before. Josie translated 'lovely' for 'desirable', understanding the feeling so well.

Josie now understood what Thomas had experienced and was fascinated by the effect Ester had had on him within such a very short period of time, without any physical contact whatever. She thought for a moment, then suggested to him that the next time he met her he should invite her to dinner, informing her that she was going to be there with her friend Mr Martin, who had been a one-time stage partner – he lived in Watling Street, just round the corner from St Paul's Churchyard. She said he should fetch Ester at six o'clock and take her home afterwards at nine, in a Hansom cab. Josie pictured the evening's party being held in the side room which was for her use only.

Thomas was all the while nodding at the ease with which Josie was going through the preparations. It all sounded so easy. Now he began to worry about whether Ester would accept the invitation or whether it had all been a fantasy in his head, and that she had never really smiled at him.

He was going to have a hard time lasting out until the following week, and he only had Saturday afternoons and Sundays off work. Was Ester going to be free? Would he find the shop empty of customers, allowing him the chance to broach the subject without the embarrassment of others overhearing? He found it quite frightening. All this and more was racing through his head, to the extent that he thought he would burst.

CHAPTER 7

The jacket

Having a new consignment of silver ingots in for melting down and then for pouring into moulds kept Thomas busy for the rest of the week. At last Saturday morning arrived. He had only some clearing up to do and to sort out the work for the following week. This would give him time to concentrate on seeing Ester and picking up his jacket in the afternoon.

Just thinking about her name excited him. It was sufficient to allow him to picture her, feel her closeness. He remembered how she had pulled down his sleeve, the way it felt when she measured the sleeve length of the jacket, having to bend down to see how long the sleeves were, allowing him for a moment to picture the swelling of her breasts under her bodice...

Enough of all that – he had to get there, and it was about time he started out. On the way he meant to post his monthly letter to his parents at the post office near St Martin's Le Grand before turning into Paternoster Row, Ludgate Hill and then Fleet Street. He always enjoyed his walk to Charing Cross. It would only take him about an hour's quick walking time to get to Queensgate. The thought of Ester spurred him on.

The London Thomas was walking through was highly discriminatory off the main roads, and awful for the poor and the multitudes of the disabled. The city fathers were unable or unwilling to tackle its problems. The streets were crowded with many different street workers. The old, narrow lanes were packed with people, and when a coach turned into it the walkers were forced to push forward, trampling children and the disabled and forcing the whole crowd to pour out at the other end into an already heavily populated area. This was happening all around London, a city that was not designed for so much daily traffic. The carts were becoming larger to accommodate heavier loads gathered from canal warehouses, and were pulled by increasingly large carthorses.

Water was not universally drunk. The street pumps were used for washing, but never for drinking. It was discoloured and smelt, the pipes often being blocked by dead rats. Beer was the usual drink for breakfast, dinner and tea for all ages. London was the centre for gin distilling, there being some 75 distilleries in the city. Sugar imported from the

West Indies was refined at the warehouse. This was a time when the outlying farms could keep up with the necessary produce with lard, oil, mustard, vinegar, chocolate and biscuits, all factory produced.

Thomas was familiar with the area around Christ's Hospital. The tenements contained many families, their washing and cleaning making the gullies in the centre of the street overflow. There was a church in every square, and in some a railing circled the graveyard.

Thomas reached Queens Gate crossroads off the Cromwell Road in good time. His aim was to get to the shop by two o'clock, and it was now five to. He was beginning to feel distinctly nervous. He had to be there to get his jacket, so there was no way round it, he had to go on. He approached the shop door, knocked and opened the door...

As he walked away from the shop a few minutes later, his pace quickened. His mind was going over the encounter. The meeting could not have gone any better, and the result had been too exciting for words. He stopped to calm himself down, and to think about her kiss. Oh my dear God, how delicious, what wonderful lips! He continued his walk back giddy with romantic thoughts.

He wondered what the chances were that he would somehow eventually win her, marry her and perhaps even have a family with her. He knew absolutely nothing about marriage and having children. The thought of lying in a bed with Ester with nothing on, feeling her body move, watching her chest breathing, her heart beating, surrendering to him, was extraordinary. He was so ignorant and innocent. Perhaps Josie would be able to set him straight and prepare him. Would she do that? Oh dear, how stupid he was! His mind kept playing tricks as he walked along. He was almost home. Perhaps he could have another word with Josie tonight about it all?

He opened the front door to let himself in. In his room, he carefully hung up his coat. He really should have a look at what Ester had done. He took the coat out and looked at the sleeves. He could make out the alterations and see how neat they were and how tiny the stitches. He could see her now, taking such care. But it was almost time for dinner. He should change.

He caught Josie just as he reached the bottom of the stairs.

"Well, how did you get on?" She looked nearly as excited as he was.

"Can I tell you later?"

"Yes, come into my sitting room after you've had your dinner." with that they both went on their way, Josie into the kitchen and Thomas to his meal.

The usual banter was being exchanged, plates rattled, drinks were poured and salt was passed. Josie's serving girl set his dinner before him. Steak and kidney pie, what could be better than that? He tucked in, finding himself more peckish than he had imagined; after all that had happened that afternoon, he was hungry.

At last the meal was over and the plates were removed. They sat back and surveyed each other. "Right," said Josie. She had been careful not to say anything during the meal to find out what had happened, as she knew she would get a far better account if she waited.

"I have been very patient," she said. "I'm longing to hear the result of your offer."

Thomas sat back, replete. He was so happy and contented, but that did not stop him from holding back, teasing Josie, taking his time. He took a sip of wine as he did so. He decided to tell his story from the very beginning, to achieve the right atmosphere and conclusion.

"I arrived on time, and the shop was empty of customers. I went in and Ester came into the shop from the workroom with my jacket over her arm. She placed it on the table. We shook hands and both said some appropriate kind words. She wanted me to try the jacket on to see if the alterations were correct, so I took off my coat. She helped me to put on the jacket, smoothing down the back, making sure the collar was raised and pulling down the sleeves. She was so close and so competent, which made me feel excited and rather nervous. The way she took control of the situation, attending to every facet of the dressing, was wonderful.

"The jacket fitted perfectly and I said so. She helped me take it off and to put my coat back on. All the time she was circling me, talking about the alterations, saying how well the jacket set off my appearance. I was in heaven, in a daze.

"Finally a moment arrived when I could invite her to

sit down and I did so. I then told her about the dinner, the timing, the coach, that you would be there with a friend looking after her every wish. I think I may have overdone it a bit, I was so eager. She was so understanding, not interrupting nor questioning, just occasionally nodding and smiling, with her head on one side looking so delightful. Initially I gabbled my words, trying to fit in all I had to say. Then she put her hands together before her lips and said "I would love to!"

"I just sat there, not uttering a word, I was so unbelievably happy. If I had tears in my eyes I would not be surprised. We both stood up together. I moved to hold her hands and kiss her and she responded. I did kiss her, thanking her for her kindness, but she put her finger over my lips to stop me talking. Then she put her hand on the back of my head, pulled it down and kissed me. Now what do you make of that? She then said again that she would love to attend the party and would be ready at five-thirty."

At the end of his recital Thomas was puffing and panting, quite lost for words.

Josie smiled. "I do believe you have cracked it. Ester sees you in her arms. That is delightful. Now we have to get over the week and prepare for the occasion."

Josie was caught up in the event. There was the meal to plan, a table to furnish, and she had to contact Rob Martin and organise the kitchen staff. She told Thomas he had to book the Hansom cab and to make sure there was a blanket in the coach, in case it rained. The week was going to be busy, for her guesthouse was full.

They left the table together. Thomas kissed her cheek. "Thank you Josie, I don't know what I would have done without you through all these years."

She could see he had tears in his eyes. "Go on, get to bed and don't be silly." She knew well enough that if she stayed there any longer, she too would be crying.

CHAPTER 8

The party

The week went by grindingly slowly. Fortunately for Thomas, the foundry section was very busy and needed his close attention. Every night as he lay in bed his last thoughts were of Ester, her face so near to his as she helped him on with his coat; he could almost reach out and touch her. Her kiss, as she held his head down, her soft, parted, warm lips pressed against his. He couldn't help smiling. Not so very long ago he had never touched a woman, let alone kissed one, and now all was his to conjure with: feel her, smell her, taste her and wrap his arms around her. He closed his eyes. He could feel her breathing, pulsating no longer. Was he frowning but experiencing a living soul? Contentedly he slept…

At last Friday night came round. He had made it, thank God. In the morning his first thoughts were of the coming event. He had booked the cab for the next afternoon at five, and he had to make sure there was going to be a blanket.

He had decided what to wear the following evening; it had to include his now altered jacket and a new pair of trousers that he hadn't worn. His waistcoat, cravat and hat completed his apparel. Now all he had to do was to get there. He had spoken with Josie, who was as excited as he was. The meal had been decided, the food ordered and the kitchen staff alerted. It was almost as if the whole guest house was raised up, expectant, teetering on the brink of something special, waiting for the long awaited guest.

Five o'clock chimed; the coach had been outside for a couple of minutes. Thomas said goodbye to Josie to let her know that all was ready and that he was off to pick up Ester. The driver knew London well, particularly the City, and Whitehouse Fashions in Harrington Gardens he knew well. He had checked everything, and all was well. He tapped the roof and they were off. The adventure was about to begin.

The pair of horses trotted along past familiar roads and city sights. Thomas, keeping station, knew it wasn't far to go as they had just passed Trafalgar Square. The horses stopped outside. This was it. Thomas gathered himself up and got out. "One minute," he told the driver. He walked up to the door, which opened to reveal Mrs Whitehouse, who stood there ready to let Thomas in. She touched his arm. "You will look after her?"

"Dear Mrs Whitehouse, I deal with precious metals and beautiful jewellery," he said. "You can rest assured I will look after Ester – she is my greatest jewel." He felt light headed. Did he just say that? He entered the shop. Ester once again walked into the room, this time dressed in blue.

Josie and Ester had had a merry time sorting through Josie's wardrobe. When the choice had been made, they discussed what alterations were necessary. The dress had the waist taken in and a few pleats added, and now it was perfect for the occasion. Trying it on afterwards, Ester looked stunning. As she walked towards him, he could hardly believe that he was the one to escort her to the coach. They held hands and turned to say goodbye to Josie, who quickly disappeared back into the shop.

Thomas helped Ester up the steps the coachman had kindly let down and into the coach. It wasn't raining, in fact the sun came out as if a light had been switched on, shining on Ester. A tap on the roof and they set off back to Aldersgate.

They turned and looked at each other. Thomas said, "You do know I love you, darling Ester?"

Ester gazed into his eyes. "Yes, I do, Thomas, I love you too."

They squeezed hands, and perhaps they had tears in their eyes. For a second there was silence as the horses clip-clopped along, then they each burst out at the same time, "You make me so happy!" They both laughed to cover up their embarrassment. It was going to be, for each of them, a day they would never forget.

They were silent all the way up to St Pauls and onwards to the guest house in Aldersgate Road. The coach pulled up outside the front door of the guest house, which immediately opened to reveal Mrs Whitehouse, who came down the steps. By this time the coachmen had descended and opened the door to allow Thomas to alight, and he offered a hand up to Ester, who stepped onto the pavement to be greeted by Josie. "Well now, there's no need for me to ask how you are, you look lovely," she said. "Now come along, both of you." She led Ester up the steps into the house.

Thomas was left to fend for himself, remembering to remind the coachman to be back for a return trip at nine-thirty to Drury Lane. With that the coachman pulled away with a wave. He too had been affected by the couple's obvious delight at being in each other's company.

Thomas caught up with Josie and Ester in the hall in perfect time to introduce Ester to Mrs Whitehouse. "Mrs Whitehouse, may I introduce you to Miss Ester Pepler from Great Stanmore."

Ester put out her hand, which was gently shaken by Josie. "Miss Pepler, may I call you Ester?"

Ester replied, "Yes please, if I may call you Josie."

"Of course you may."

"Well Ester, I have looked forward so much to our meeting. I have heard nothing but wonderful things about you from Thomas – he never ceases to proclaim his delight at meeting you."

"Now now, Josie," said Thomas. "You are right in what you say, but you'll embarrass Ester."

Ester burst out laughing. “Josie, I love Thomas, and whatever he does pleases me.”

Josie had never met anyone so joyous and fresh, and was almost embarrassed by her casual matter-of-fact openness. “Well I never Thomas, many congratulations are due. Now everyone, come and meet my other guest.”

With that, Jodie took Ester’s hand and guided her through the guest’s dining room to her own sitting room beyond, where the table had been laid for four. A man sitting down on a sofa leapt to his feet.

“Now Ester, May I, introduce you to Mr Steven James, who is stage manager at the Opera House.”

Steven thrust out his hand. “Enchanted my dear, please call me Steven.”

Josie continued, “Steven, this is Thomas Kearey, the fortunate man Ester loves.” Both men shook hands, laughing. “Please Ester, sit here.” Thomas lifted out the chair for Ester to sit on, then moved it back in.

“Now Thomas, you sit over there opposite Ester whilst I sit here,” said Josie. Steven held the back of her chair with accomplished skill whilst Josie sat down. Taking the remaining chair, Josie sat down and looked around her guests. “You are my favourite people, celebrating Thomas and Ester meeting each other. I hope we all remain friends forever. Now let me ring the bell.” A little table bell was shaken, the door opened and in came one of the serving girls with the first course on a tray. She was followed by another holding an open bottle, who stood back whilst the plates were distributed. She then passed round the table, pouring out the sparkling wine. "Thank you," said Josie to the staff. With that, they left the four waiting for Josie to lift up her glass to bless the occasion. Then the momentous evening began.

The conversation moved backwards and forwards as the meal progressed. They were all interested in Ester's move down to London and her training and friendship with Rose Springer, Josie's previous life on stage and Steven's experience managing opera companies. But most of all the company wanted to hear about Thomas' previous life as a young man in Dublin and his home life there. It was naturally Ester who pressed him most to describe how tough he had had to be to take the enormous step to work in London.

Thomas explained the act of Union in 1801 between Ireland and England, how Catholics would be allowed to stand for Parliament and take part in appointing judges, only to find later that there was no way the middle and upper classes, who were in the main Protestants, would allow that to happen. On the land farmers could be evicted at the will of the landlord, usually at the end of a lease or if no lease was available at six months' notice. His parents and friends applauded his strength of character to strike out in London. Those round the table did so too. Ester looked at him in a new light. Thomas had been in London for seven years, learning to fit in, to learn a business and make friends. Now he was in love with her, and it showed.

Thomas was surprised at his own feelings. Yes, it was true that he wanted to become a Londoner. Now he had achieved that, and had papers to prove it, he was thinking about getting married and taking the responsibility of a wife and perhaps children. He would have to house them, educate them and protect them, in fact do everything in his power to see that they had the best childhoods possible, so that all that could be passed on would be, for the generations to follow, so that they should know about their Irish past and the hereditary history of the clan.

CHAPTER 9

Ester's family

The Pepler family were well-known villagers in Great Stanmore, and had been so for generations. Edward Pepler (b. 1774) was the village provider of firewood for the big house. In spare moments he repaired fences and field boundaries. His wife Mary (née Collins) raised chickens, selling both the birds and their eggs to augment Edward's seasonal pay. The couple's daughters Ester (b. 1794) and younger sister Hester attended the village school, at the cost of a 1d per day for each child; they also attended Sunday school, where their mother taught a class of five. There were very few villagers who did not know the Peplers, who were known as 'the hen house family.'

The estate was owned by James Brydges, 1st Duke of Chandos, a British landowner and politician who sat in the House of Commons from 1698 until 1714. When he succeeded to the peerage as Baron Chandos, he vacated his seat in the Commons to sit in the House of Lords. He was subsequently created Earl of Carnarvon. In the Middle-Ages, a monastic community, or cell of Augustinian Canons, was established at Bentley Priory. It was dissolved in 1536 during the Dissolution of the Monasteries. The Canons ward, which covers the eastern areas, had a population of 12,471 in the later 1841 census.

The area was recorded in the Domesday Book as Stanmere, the name deriving from the Old English words 'stan' for stony and 'mere', a pool'. In 1841, Great Stanmore was a parish of 1,441. It was roughly the shape of an elongated rectangle, running from north-north-west to south-south-east. The village lay at its centre, 10 miles from London.

Stanmore was divided, before the Norman Conquest, into estates foreshadowing the later parishes of Great and Little Stanmore. The name of Great Stanmore does not occur until 1354. Village life for both women and men was busy, strenuous and continuous. Their diet was poor, dress simple and housing primitive. Sanitary arrangements were all outside and little better than a bucket. Relationships continued, love, sex and marriage; neighbours quarrelled and fought each other, knew each other intimately and in the end depended on each other, especially for ploughing and harvesting. It was a system that suited the simple life. The landowners were content to leave things as they were; change, when it did come along, was from outside the village, usually by a new landowner or by someone used to town life.

Throughout its history the main settlement, to which there was no equivalent in Little Stanmore, was often called just Stanmore. The parish was limited to a few natural features or roads. Its northern boundary crossed Bushey Heath, where the boundaries of the manors of Great Stanmore and Bushey were surveyed in 1595. The inclusion of Stanmore marsh and farm on Whitchurch Lane was not finally determined, by agreement with Little Stanmore, until the 1820s. The workhouse, close upon both Day's and Atkinsons Alms-Houses, were close to the Independent's Chapel on the St Albans Road, close to Stone Grove. After that time the eastern boundary, running from Hertfordshire along the west side of Cloisters wood to the bottom of Dennis Lane, continued south down Marsh Lane and bulged outwards at Stanmore marsh before heading almost as far south as the village of Queensbury.

The southern boundary with Harrow, Hatch End and Headstone runs for a short way along Honeypot Lane before turning west a little to the south of modern Streatfield Road. The western boundary, also with Harrow, was later marked by a line slightly east of Uppingham Avenue, curving north-west towards Vernon Drive, where it crossed Belmont, a mound constructed by James Brydges. Stanmore Park, the Uxbridge road and the grounds of Bentley Priory all lie east of the mansion, to finally reach Hertfordshire, where Magpie Hall Road meets Heathbourne Road.

The list of prominent people from the area includes John Warner (d. 1565), physician, William Wigan Harvey (1810-83), divine son of George Daniel Harvey of Montagues, were natives of the parish. General Robert Burne died in retirement at Berkeley Cottage, Stanmore, in 1825. Charles Hart (d. 1683), Baptist Minister Wriothesley Noel (1798-1873), and Arthur Hamilton-Gordon (1829-1912), colonial governor, also residents.

In the Middle Ages the busiest road ran from Watling Street, the old Roman Road, to Watford. The section which entered from Little Stanmore, probably near the crest of the ridge at Spring Pond, was rendered useless in the early 18th century by the Duke of Chandos' diversions around Canons, but the north-western stretch was left to follow the old route along the edge of Stanmore Common and on into Harrow parish.

At the bottom of the ridge a lesser route cut south-westwards through the parish, linking Watling Street with Harrow Weald and Uxbridge. It followed the line of the modern Broadway and Church Road, continuing between the sites of the existing church and the rectory along Colliers Lane before that stretch was reduced by the building of Stanmore Park; later Uxbridge Road, a 'new' road in 1800, was laid out with its bulge to the north. Across it ran two ways from the high ground: Dennis Lane, which joined it at the boundary and continued south as Marsh Lane, Honeypot Lane, and Green Lane. The second continued south as Old Church Lane before turning east to meet Marsh Lane, then known as Watery Lane, which itself turned to join Honeypot Lane. Dennis Lane, so called by 1578, and its southerly extensions give a north to south trackway older than Watling Street; the route along Green and Old Church Lanes, mentioned respectively in 1580 and 1633, led to the main medieval settlement.

Little Stanmore in 1800 was a parish in the union of Hendon, 'Hundreds of Gore,' county of Middlesex, half a mile northwest from Edgware, containing 830 inhabitants. The living was a perpetual curacy, in the gift of the Armstrong family: the great tithes commuted for £36.10d, and the incumbent's for £415.

Ester lived with her parents in Dennis Lane. Each of the cottages had its own particular name. All the lanes and roads were colloquially known as "The Street." Each cottage looked different, all built around their chimneys, as if they needed the chimneys to keep them standing. The brickwork, stained and rubbed, looked like stone. All the gardens had their own vegetable patches, chicken runs, woodsheds and washing outhouses; in this they were little different from outlying parishes throughout rural Britain.

The road called Stanmore Hill, reaching the Uxbridge road between Dennis Lane and Green Lane, may have started as a branch from Green Lane, which it meets halfway up the slope. Since the 18th century, Stanmore Hill has also been the name for the old stretch of road between that fork and the top of the ridge. Following the Duke of Chandos' buildings around Canons Park, most travellers from Watford descended Stanmore Hill before meeting those coming from Uxbridge. East of the junction, at the bottom of Dennis Lane, they could reach the old Roman road of Watling Street by taking the new London road straight across Little Stanmore or by going south down Marsh Lane before turning into Whitchurch Lane.

The church school taught 24 children. In 1713 there was a collection made for it, and the money gathered, with some contributions from London, where an unknown gentleman gave £5, enabled the trustees to clothe all the children for the first time.

The master of the workhouse was made responsible for teaching paupers' children. £80 was borrowed from the funds of the Sunday school and by 1798, a schoolroom was built in the workhouse. Ester Pepler left school in the summer of 1808, having turned fourteen that July. She could read and write. The schoolmaster or school dame had received three shillings for every boy or girl taught to know all the letters of the alphabet, but only when so taught. He or she was to receive six shillings for each child who could spell English, eleven shillings for each child who could read English and say the catechism perfectly.

The second part of the charity was for boys only, for ten boys from the parishes to write well, cast accounts and understand the five fundamental rules of arithmetic. For each boy the master or mistress received £1.12s by stages, having to provide each boy with pen, ink and paper. The boys from ten to fourteen, after two years, chosen to receive £2 to be apprenticed to a trade. Each child received an indenture of apprenticeship, to be signed by two Justices of the Peace. The girls were taught to knit, spin and make bone lace.

Ester's parents saw an advertisement for a young girl to train to become a seamstress. Wishing to promote Ester into a more forward-looking society, they made an application, which was accepted. The acceptance letter set out her duties, what she would be taught, her hours and what she should wear. There was nothing about what she would be paid, then or later. Training was to take place the following year if the preceding year's work had been completed satisfactorily.

The shop's premises were near the church and Harrington crossroads in Queens Gate, Old Brompton. The Imperial Institute and the Natural History Museum were over the other side of Cromwell Road, and these drew in shoppers and visitors to all the merchants and houses around.

Mrs Springer's gowns and suits clothed both men and women. Ester was not going to be trained until the following year, having first to clean and tidy up the sewing room daily, fold up and put away the material not required, and familiarise herself with the work in progress, the methods used and the work tables necessary for each job. In essence, she had to fetch and carry, be in attendance when necessary and show keenness during for her first year. She was looking forward to having the responsibility.

The horses snorted and brayed as they galloped forward, taking Ester to the place where she would begin work for Mrs Springer. She felt scared as the coach bobbed and swayed and negotiated the uneven road surface, but she did not intend to show it. She was feeling very grown up, sitting in the London coach looking out of the window and waving goodbye as she passed her school friends. They were now on holiday, while she was off to work in London on her own, the very first time she had left home without her parents.

The coachmen had been spoken to quietly by Mr and Mrs Pepler, who kindly asked him to look after their daughter and to make sure she left the coach at Charing Cross and was passed over to Mrs Springer, who would be there to meet them. Thankfully the time for the coach to be in Charing Cross was generally kept, at least to within half an hour.

Ester had been carefully told what was expected of her, why they were sending her away, and what the benefits would be for her if she did as she was told. She was polite and conscientious in all things, as she would be throughout her life, and her parents believed very little harm would come to her. She was the perfect picture of a young lady of the time and looked it – petite and charming.

CHAPTER 10

Ester leaves home

Ester's first year was to be an introductory one. At fourteen, she had just left a Church School, later to become a National School, established in 1811, which taught an elementary curriculum both standardised and repetitive; the pupils were drilled by a number of exercises recited by rote, many sung first thing in the morning; her writing exercises given the same repetitive teaching using a slate and chalk. The older children taught the beginners, giving them responsibility and leadership qualities.

Ester had never been away from home and was to experience loneliness and fear, wondering if she would ever see her parents again. Great Stanmore was tiny compared to living in London with all its new distractions and surroundings, but Mrs Springer was determined to give Ester the very best home life possible, remembering loneliness in her own childhood. Teaching this young girl to be a seamstress able to design and make her own dresses was something she was quite able to do, but first she had to explain and teach a totally new standard of toiletry, eating and living so that Ester would fit in and not feel a stranger. Mrs Springer knew that Ester would find it all very different at first – getting to know her routine and the shop workers' daily habits. Ester was going to have to be patient and amenable to become used to living somewhere else, become acquainted with her surroundings both indoors and out, and to understand the shop's clothing business, staff and customers.

The training which would come in her second year involved being shown different stitches and their uses, materials necessary for the type of work ordered, hems to be turned up and secured, lace for cuffs and collars, lining up and stitching, buttons, ribbons and laces sewn on squarely and securely. The following year she was expected to start cutting out and to learn to follow a pattern.

Mrs Springer owned the Lace and Bobbin milliners and gown shop in the Old Brompton Road on or near Queens Gate Church. She was able to put Ester in one of the upstairs rooms. The shop front was open onto the pavement, allowing customers to walk straight in. The Georgian windows allowed customers to look inside and see the dummies used for modelling the gowns and suits.

As time went by, Ester began to call Mrs Springer Rosie. In 1812 Ester had become a beautiful eighteen-year-old. She had been with Mrs Springer's fashion shop for four years, and was fast becoming fully trained in hand work, though not in the latest changes in fashion. She had become a friend and confidante of Rosie Springer, and they spent a lot of time in each-other's company. Rosie tended to look upon Ester as her daughter. They were living in the same house, over the shop, sharing the same facilities but not the costs. Rosie paid Ester a small wage whilst paying for everything else. Rosie acted very much like a companion, rather than a worker, and the two other dress and suit makers accepted her as a competent member of staff.

On the Saturday afternoon when Thomas walked into the shop, it appeared empty until Ester walked in from the room beyond, asking if she could help. Thomas asked Ester, "Is it possible to have a jacket altered?" Ester said it would be possible, and Thomas fished his best jacket out of his bag. Ester asked Thomas, "Please put the jacket on and tell me how you would like it to be altered." With that Thomas took off his coat and put on the jacket and for the first time, he looked at Ester, catching her smiling at his shyness. He had never seen such a lovely-looking woman standing so close to him before, even when dancing.

He drew in his breath. "I would very much like the sleeves shortened, if that is at all possible?"

Ester pulled down the sleeves and walked round him looking at him from every angle. This was a new experience.

Fetching a chalk disc, she made some guiding marks to reduce the length of the sleeves by half an inch to allow the undershirt cuffs to show. "Would this suit you?" she said. He would have agreed to anything, and he nervously replied, "That's perfect." He was captivated by her.

Ester put the jacket aside saying, "I could have this ready for next week, if that's acceptable. I can start tomorrow – make it a priority."

"That's fine, can you give me the probable cost?"

Ester thought carefully about what she was going to say, not wanting to do the job, hand it over and never see him again. "I charge by the hour, which is a shilling. This should take about two hours." She knew perfectly well that there was every chance it was going to take longer than that.

"That's lovely," said Thomas.

"Oh, by the way, do you mind if I have your name in case you are not here when I come in?" he said. She answered. "Not at all, that is quite in order. It's Ester."

"Till next week then."

Ester, in turn wanting to know his name, requested it for the firm's book. She held out a book and a pencil, and he carefully wrote down his name and address. She watched him, noticing how he moved. Was this impersonal, or was she more than just interested? She admitted to herself that she was. Thomas was tall, handsome and well built. He had a pleasant, pleasing manner and was genteel in a strong, manly way. The more she thought about it, the more breathless she became. She felt herself flushing. Oh dear, what a spectacle she was making! This was the first time she had ever felt and behaved less than professionally. Who could blame her? All her life she had done as she was told quite willingly, without questioning what she was doing or why. Now she was questioning herself. She wanted a man to show interest in her and what she was doing, to make her to feel important, not in a powerful way but because she was a woman who wanted to feel safe, needed and sexual. This was the first time such a thought, or even such a word, had entered her mind, but yes, she did indeed want to be sexual.

She smiled to herself. Now she could play with her thoughts about him, the way he walked and talked, his softness and gentleness as he took the paper and pencil. She could feel she was aroused. *Oh dear, this will never do, I had better get on*, she thought.

PART 3

CHAPTER 11

The invitation

After Thomas had left the shop, Ester read the name again: Thomas Kearey. Even his name was attractive. She mentally repeated it, then looked up, surprised by her feelings. The way he spoke he didn't sound like a local person at all, but he was obviously educated and very good looking. She couldn't wait to tell Rosie.

The following morning Ester came into the shop well before Rosie, who was still at her home going through business paperwork. Ester wasn't bothered to find herself early. She started to prepare the shop for customers, tidying up the previous day's work, then immediately got on with shortening the sleeves, feeling the jacket's warmth and softness, very conscious that this was the coat Thomas had put on.

The more Ester tried to keep Thomas out of her mind, the more he came back into it. "Lord," she exclaimed to herself, "how pleased I'm going to be to get this matter off my chest and to have somebody else to talk to about it!" With that she sat back to await Rosie, but she found herself still holding onto the coat. Perhaps she ought to put it down; that might take Thomas out of her head.

It wasn't long before a rattle of keys in the lock announced the arrival of Rosie. "Well Ester, you have set my mind a-buzzing. Now, what have you been up to?"

This was Ester's chance to clear her mind and involve Rosie, who after all was far more experienced in life, having been married and being three times Ester's age and with a business to look after. "Well, it was like this…"

Ester made the most of the story of her meeting with Thomas. Every little moment, word and deed was articulated, relished and highly coloured. Rosie sat quite still, entranced by Ester's description, thinking back to her own life as an eighteen-year-old attracted to a man for the first time, not knowing how to behave or how to show enough interest to invite another meeting without showing desperation.

At last Ester paused for breath and stared at Rosie with her mouth open. "That's it, all of it."

Rosie exclaimed. "You say he's coming in a week today to collect his jacket?"

"Yes, in the afternoon." Rosie anticipated Thomas' state of mind, recognising that Ester was extremely attractive and pleasant to all her customers, and had a very easy manner and a charming voice. What single man would not want to renew her acquaintance?

"Well dear, I believe Thomas has to come back for his jacket and is very likely he will try to make advances, perhaps even to ask you out," she said. "It's up to you to show interest and to agree to see him again out of working hours, at a time which suits you both, preferably when there are friends around to make the occasion less stressful."

Ester drew breath, and revealed all to Rosie about her meeting. Telling the story did clear her mind, and it opened up a deeply held longing suppressed for years. She would like to have a man friend who wanted her as a companion for life, someone who would protect her, comfort her and love her.

As soon as she had said this to herself, she stopped again. Yes, she wanted to be loved, physically loved and made complete, to have her body admired, to have it touched and to experience every sensuous emotion. She had read about such things and had also imagined having a baby of her own at her breast. She did want her own children, children who would look to her as their mother, to feed them, and for the child to look to her for comfort and security. These things had been suppressed in her, but now she had found her own security in Rosie.

Without over-indulging herself, she looked up at Rosie and smiled. "Well there you are, I shall have to contain myself until next Saturday afternoon with only his jacket as a comforter." She laughed, giggled and went red.

The shop door opened, the bell jangled, and there was Thomas. The previous week had not been a dream after all. He looked as beautiful as her memory pictured him. *Oh God, let this be all right, may my dreams come true.* She smiled and moved towards him, nearly tripping over the chair that held his coat. "Good afternoon, the jacket's all ready for you," she said.

Thomas stepped towards her, holding out his hand. Ester took it and pressed it, looking into his face and smiling. He voiced his thoughts. "It's lovely to see you again and to hear about the jacket. Perhaps I might try it on?" He raised his eyebrows.

"Of course," she said. "I have it just here ready for you."

He knew very well the jacket would be fine; he just wanted Ester to be near him again. Ester picked up the jacket and held it up for him to slip his arms into the sleeves. He turned round to face her and held out his arms as if to test the sleeves' lengths. She stood close to him after placing the jacket over his shoulders. Thomas turned, his arms still outstretched, accidentally touching her arms. She did not back away but stood there with her head on one side, smiling.

Thomas now smiled too and closed his hand over her arm. "Please excuse me, I so wanted to see you again – the week has just lasted forever and now my hopes are before me, you are no more a dream but a beautiful reality." He let his hands drop. "May I have a word?"

They faced each other. Ester wanted Thomas to feel

welcomed and happy, not shy or nervous but at ease. "Please sit down, Thomas," she said. He waited for her to take a chair, then he too sat down. Now be began to recite what Rosie had suggested.

"Ester, I very much wanted to see you again to invite you out to dinner next Saturday, to my lodgings, if you can make it? It will allow me to introduce you to my friend and her gentleman friend, to enjoy a special dinner together. I can come in a hackney carriage to pick you up at six and return you at say nine. Please say you would like to come?"

Tears came into her eyes. Her dream was becoming reality. An evening specially prepared with a chaperone, the whole event planned to perfection; she could not fault it. She shifted in her chair, looked Thomas straight in the eye and replied, "That sounds wonderful. Yes, I would very much like to come to your party."

Thomas was enraptured. The invitation, the acceptance and Ester's whole bearing were exactly what he had hoped for. Throughout the previous week he had mentally gone through this moment. All though the later stages of his apprenticeship, holding fast during the training afterwards, he had listened to the most negative voices talking about the lives his fellow countrymen and women were leading throughout Ireland. He had pushed that aside, planning to make a better life and having to keep on working hard to make his skills ever more appropriate for his work, making sure his efforts would not be wasted. Now here was the prize. He must not foul it up but keep steadfast and sure he knew he had been right. Ester was all that he had hoped for – his dreams were coming true.

He looked up. "That's settled then. I shall be here at six. Thank you." He stood up, took her hand to help her stand, and kissed her. "Please forgive me, I am so happy."

Ester laughed. "That allows me to kiss you, for I'm so happy too."

"Oh, by the way I had better pay you." He handed over the money. "Goodbye Ester, keep safe, I will not let you down."

It was time to leave. Once again he couldn't wait to get home and tell Rosie all about it. "Till next Saturday then." He gathered up his jacket and opened the door, looking back at Ester. "Bye, my dear!" He walked away as if in a dream. How wonderful life was! Now, what should he wear?

Ester thought through every second of the afternoon's meeting, going over every moment, movement and nuance. It had lived up to all her dreams. Before going to sleep she had painted this picture in her mind. In fact she turned over in bed to look into his eyes, reaching out her hand to touch him, her imagination so strong that she was sure he was there.

Thomas had been kind, gentle and accommodating. She did not know who or what his employer was or what he did, nor did she know the position Thomas' finances were in, what job security he had, and if he had any vices or social ills. She knew what her position would be if she left

Rosie Springer and the shop. She had limited savings and very little to fall back on, with no family living nearby. She would have to totally rely upon Thomas. Her next talk with Rosie was going to be difficult.

CHAPTER 12

Preparations for a party

The evening meal was being prepared by Rosie, as it was her turn at the stove. Ester laid the table, tidied the room and lit the fire. It had become a habit to swap all the tasks. At the very beginning of their relationship, when Ester had first been employed, she had followed Rosie around watching everything she did, how she did it and in what order. The training had soon been completed, and Ester matched her skills at working with different dress materials and styles. Rosie left it to her to decorate the windows, finding she had far more design ability than she had for the job. Theirs were an easy and pleasant relationship, one born out of necessity for both. Rosie however was in her sixties and would be retiring soon; she was not too good on her legs.

That evening was going to be interesting for them, and they would both have to be frank. Ester knew she was in danger of getting ahead of herself. She had to think of her future and plan ahead, but not if it was going to ruin her relationship with Rosie, which was all important. Rosie was now her protector and backbone.

Rosie shouted down, "Right Ester, dinner is served." Omelette and salad, perfect, thought Ester. The two women sat down, passing each other the plates and condiments. "Now Ester, in your own time, describe this afternoon with Thomas," said Rosie

"Well firstly, the afternoon went very well. Thomas was happy with the alterations. What was most interesting was that he invited me to a private dinner party, with his guesthouse owner, and friend. What do you think?"

"That sounds all right, carry on."

"The party is going to be held in my honour, at his lodgings in Aldersgate. He suggested picking me up by coach next Saturday at five-thirty, then returning at nine-thirty. He was so excited and happy I just could not refuse. I accepted. I do hope that's all right. I can easily cancel though, he left me his address. He was so charming and considerate and I really like him and his manner. I am so inexperienced, I know so little of etiquette. Will I be all right? You have been so kind to me looking after me like a mother. I never want to leave you, I would miss you so. But Thomas' attention has stirred up within me a desire for love, to physically touch another person – a man. Is that so unnatural or dangerous?"

"My dear Ester what you are experiencing is natural, and something everyone experiences. It's not dangerous if you keep it all within bounds. Never express any inner feelings which are not true, for it will come back and haunt you. Just think carefully what you are doing, for your own inner being will tell you if you are doing wrong or the situation is becoming dangerous. Don't be afraid of telling Thomas what you believe, how you see the world, and how you would like him to treat you. If he is right for you he will respond with kindness and compassion."

Rosie had listened hard and pictured the couple going through normal courting behaviour: the nervousness, the hopes and fears, the longings and desires. It was all very exciting, but she also knew that in life there were many upsets and demands just round the corner, threatening unhappiness. Ester was so natural, kind and forgiving, the sort of person Rosie had wished for as a daughter, but it had never happened; she was childless. Now she had her friend Ester to live through, and what was happening now had been bound to happen sooner or later. She could not be unkind and put a damper on the fire of possible love.

"I think it will be fine," she said. "I've listened to your description of the meeting and I'm pleased that Thomas has included a chaperone to make you less afraid. He has set a limited time for the first occasion and a respectable time to return you home. I believe you should go and enjoy yourself and put all fears and worries to one side."

"Oh Rosie," she said, with tears in her eyes. "I am so happy with life. I have you, and now a man friend, someone who likes me well enough to plan a special party for! I believe he is as affected as I am by the way he kept fiddling with his cravat."

Rosie thought for a moment, then said, "I have never known you to be unkind or to do anything to hurt others. I have done my best to guide you and teach you how to reach out for all the best things in life, those things that are natural and free. To walk in the garden or the park and notice the trees and shrubs grow through the different seasons. Well that is the same for us; you are going through different seasons too, which will make you grow. Having you live with me and in effect become my daughter has been good for me, for I have grown stronger with each passing year instead of growing weaker with old age. So I have as much to be thankful for."

This was all so unlike Ester's normal behaviour, which was normally cool, calm, and collected. She had become affected by the occasion, revealing her innermost feelings and thoughts that had remained dormant for so long. She was opening up, becoming susceptible to Thomas' innocent invitation.

"What should I wear?" It was af question all young women ask at their first date.

Rosie smiled. "I believe I have the perfect outfit. It just needs a little altering. Perhaps you would like to see it?"

The two set off to wash and put away the dinner things before making their way upstairs for Ester to try on dresses. Rosie looked on.

It was an obvious choice, a pale blue dress. Ester's own work on it made it even tighter fitting round the waist, using numerous pleats to emphasise her breasts. She looked at herself in the mirror. Yes, she was happy with that. Ever since Thomas had kissed her and declared his love for her, she had fantasised about her future. She did want to get married; she did want children. And she did want her own hom,e and yes she did want to look after Rosie, who had been so good to her, acting very much like a mother.

On that Saturday late afternoon, she and Rosie sat down in the shop waiting for Thomas and the coach to appear. They had gone over her meetings with him, and they had talked endlessly about what Ester wanted out of life and the steps that were going to be necessary to achieve it. Being in love with Thomas, respecting his manliness and his motives, including having to leave his parents, brother and sisters to achieve his goals, were noble things. The fact that he was attractive, tall, and good looking was a definite plus. But it was his courtesy, his charm and thoughtfulness which clinched the matter. She would be foolish to turn him down. It was unlikely that such an opportunity would come again.

CHAPTER 13

Band of gold

Just as five thirty came round, there was a knock on the shop front door. It was time to put in an appearance. The women stood up and Rosie went to the door and opened it. There stood Thomas. It did not take many seconds to see why Ester was so smitten; he was all that she had described. “Come in please, Ester is ready,” said Rosie.

Ester had meanwhile made her way to the door, collecting her bag and white silk wrap. “Thomas, how lovely to see you, and in perfect time,” she said.

They stepped outside to meet the coach. The coachman opened the door, folded down the steps, and Ester mounted them and sat down. Thomas followed to sit opposite. When the coachman had closed the coach door, Thomas moved over to sit next to her.

"I hope you don't mind my sitting next to you?"

"No, not at all, I've wanted you to, in fact, I have wanted to see you and to be with you all week."

Thomas turned his head and tapped the roof of the coach to tell the coachman to start the journey back to Drury Lane. He kept his head turned, looking at her. She looked stunningly beautiful, her lovely face smiling and her eyes shining. He was completely bowled over. She had been beautiful before, but now she captivated him completely.

The coach stopped outside the dress shop. The coachman got to the ground, opened the door and put the steps down, assisting Ester to alight.

"Thank you," she said.

The coachman turned to Thomas, who took out his purse and paid him, then escorted Ester to the door of the shop. It opened to reveal Rosie standing there inviting them in.

"Good evening, Rosie," said Thomas as he handed over Ester. "We‘ve had a lovely time, thanks to you. Please excuse me, I have decided to walk home. I have a lot to think about and the walk will do me good. May I call on Ester next Saturday, perhaps two-thirty? To have a walk in Lincoln Inn Fields and perhaps Grey's Inn Gardens. Perhaps you might like to come along with us? In any event, I will see you next week. Goodbye my darling Ester, and to you Rosie." He bowed, turned and walked back to Drury Lane, then he turned and waved. "Good bye," he called.

As he walked, he went over every second of the evening. It had proved to be in every way exactly as he had hoped.

Ester had enjoyed it, as was the aim. He had to admit to himself that she was a delight. Never in a million years would he have thought that the events of last few months could happen to him. He was so inexperienced, not knowing how he should court a beautiful woman. He did not want to be thought clumsy or crude. He brushed the thought aside, as he knew that Ester was not that sort of individual. She was thoughtful and charming, and he had to admit that she seemed to be in love with him. There was no way he was going to upset her or let her down. He would write to his parents to explain it all.

Thomas and Ester had committed themselves to a life together, but they were not, as yet, formally displaying that decision with a ring. Thomas meant to put that right. He knew he should get in touch with Ester's father and seek his permission, but distance and time made that difficult. He was sure however that Ester wanted her life to be properly regulated by etiquette for such matters. He would leave that to her. He had to become engaged, and that meant supplying a ring and performing the age-old declaration whilst fitting it to Ester's finger.

He had continued to send a letter home monthly. Both John and Elizabeth were well aware of his intentions to become engaged to Ester and to marry her. He had explained in detail her circumstances, and they thoroughly approved. They told Thomas that they would be very unlikely to attend, but emphasised how grateful they were that he wrote such informative, reliable letters, and sent him their love.

To achieve completion, an engagement ring had to be purchased. Working in a jeweller's handling precious metals and stones was convenient, and it was going to be his first task that week. He knew just the person to see. W. Bryer's chief jewellery designer, William Nash, was not to know that Thomas would be making a bee-line to his office the next day.

Thomas got dressed that Monday morning knowing that the office was already full of orders. He had told nobody else what he intended doing, not because he feared rejection but out of respect for Ester. The weekend's date, to walk in Lincoln's Inn gardens, where Thomas was hoping to propose, was not going to leave much time to offer up the ring and ask for her hand in marriage.

"Good morning Thomas," called Rosie as he descended the stairs. She was up too.

They looked at each other, thinking about the weekend party. "I cannot get over how lovely Ester is," she said.

Thomas smiled. "I did tell you." He was totally enraptured by her. God, how lucky he was! He quickly sat down to his breakfast. This was to be a significant day, one to be remembered all his life.

After breakfast he walked along Fleet Street, past all the newspaper printers and stalls. None of it distracted him. He was on a mission with a purpose, one that he had thought about. Although he was trying not to, he did allow himself to mentally touch Ester and kiss her lips. How he got to work he would never know, having his mind so stimulated, so filled with images of Ester, sitting opposite, seeing every move, grasping at every word or movement.

At last the familiar building came in sight. He made for William Turner's desk and workshop. Luckily Bill was there looking at that day's newspaper. "Hello Thomas, you're up bright and early, what's up?"

Thomas had already prepared in his mind what he was going to say. Knowing Bill was a dedicated member of staff and not an idle gossiper, he was going to have to open up and tell him the facts.

"Well Bill, it's like this." Thomas spilled the beans, going over the weekend and what was to come.

"Good gracious Thomas, you have been busy, now I understand why you are so tensed up, and what's causing it. Many congratulations! It could not have happened to a nicer fellow. You have no need to worry, we have many suitable rings and if you like we can have a look at them sometime this week. Meanwhile I'll fish out one or two which I think might be appropriate."

"That's very kind, thank you. I knew once you got to hear about my news you would be sympathetic. Now I must get back to business." He left Bill picking up the newspaper again.

Later that day Bill contacted Thomas, telling him that he had put aside a number of rings that might be suitable, if he would like to look at them. Thomas put down his pen. "Right Bill, I'm with you."

They returned to Bill's desk. Opening up the office safe,

Bill reached for a small bag and brought it to his desk. "There, see what you think."

Thomas upturned the bag and poured out the rings. They all looked beautiful as he lined them up. Some had single gemstones, others were in clusters. Some gems were decorated with a design, perhaps a leaf or flower, others set in a circle more like a small crown. Thomas pictured Ester, trying to imagine what she would prefer; something spectacular or plain? Delicate or impressive? He plumped for a simple, single diamond set in the centre of a knot design in gold.

"Do you know, I guessed you would choose that one," said Bill. "It's undoubtedly the best one there, based on a traditional Scandinavian design. You will automatically receive a reduction. It's £50, and if I may say so, it's well worth the money."

"In that case, how could I refuse?" said Thomas. He put it in a small drawstring bag Bill had given him. "Thanks Bill, I'm indebted." Now he had to find out if it fitted.

The rest of the day went by quickly. Thomas' plans had to go to the back of his mind as he went through the firm's books, checking orders and deliveries. He knew Bryers' only kept going through orders made by letter or by personal visits. Their chief profits were from waste material bought in to be turned into delicate jewellery.

Six o'clock arrived, time to go home. Thomas packed up his bag, tapping his pocket again to make sure the ring was still there. It was almost as if he were ringing a bell to

Ester's shop. His mind drew a picture of his last meeting. She had stood silhouetted by the shop's lighting, outlining her delectable shape as she waved goodbye. These thoughts lasted him back to Drury Lane and home. He had decided to show Josie the ring.

He walked up the steps and went into the hall, where he saw a pile of cases and bags. Obviously someone was coming to stay. He could hear voices, and then Josie and another woman came through the sitting room door. "Hello Thomas, let me introduce you to Beatrice Dodds," said Josie. "She's coming here to stay, she's moving in."

Thomas stepped forward, thrusting out his hand. Beatrice tilted her head, which was covered in a wide-brimmed hat. "Hello Thomas, lovely to meet you," she said. He could see Josie smiling behind her. He could tell, now smiling to himself, Beatrice was going to liven up the evening dinners. He would have to delay talking to Josie about the ring until he could catch her on her own.

He went upstairs to change for dinner, unload his bags and try to catch up with the news. Reading the daily newspaper had now become a habit. Initially he had never bothered, but not knowing the news stymied conversation during the meal, which had been embarrassing. Thinking back, he realised how much he had changed. A few years ago he had known nothing about London, its streets, shops, houses and people. Now he knew them intimately. He knew their fears and temptations, their needs and their daily wants, their conversation, songs and dances. He was surprised at himself. He was becoming a Londoner without knowing it.

The dinner bell rang, and he put the paper down, put on his jacket and went downstairs. He was one of the first to enter the dining room. Gradually the table filled. The waitresses brought in the dinner and passed round the plates, seeing that everyone was being served.

There was some desultory conversation, but in main the guests were busy eating, occasionally passing the condiments or the water jug. The news of the day would wait until the guests sat back in their chairs and lit up their cigars, perhaps even passing round the port. Thomas, well used to the procedure conformed, respecting the pleasant dinner routine. After a short period the guests left the table to go upstairs or take a stroll outside. He took this opportunity to waylay Josie as she passed through.

"Come with me" she said, indicating with a crooked finger that he was to follow her into her private sitting room. She turned round and signalled for him to sit.

"Right, tell me all about it," she said.

"Well," said Thomas, "I've proposed and Ester's accepted. I have chosen a ring and on Saturday I am going to propose to her and offer it to her for her approval. I haven't asked her father, but I'm sure Ester will. I will write to him too and explain the circumstances, and beg his forgiveness." With that he fished out the little drawstring bag, got up and gave it to her.

She opened the bag and looked at the ring. "My, this is

a wonderful ring. I'm sure she will love it and wear it with pride."

Thomas let out a sigh. "Thank goodness for that. I hoped you might like it, and could see it on her finger. Now all I have to do is wait with bated breath for Saturday afternoon and see."

The day arrived, and once again, Thomas walked all the way, only this time he went down Long Acre to Leicester Square, Piccadilly Circus, Green Park, around Hyde Park corner, and on down Cromwell Road. He was looking forward to proposing, but most of all, holding Ester and kissing her.

He checked his pocket again; there it was, a small delicate stone that meant so much, because it would bring the two of them together for life. He knocked on the door of the shop; Rosie opened it and beckoned him in.

"Hello Thomas. Lovely to see you. I'm sure these walks do you a power of good."

"Yes, they do indeed. They are also very revealing about the state of people's housing and all the new advances that are being brought in to improve London's employment and social conditions."

CHAPTER 14

The proposal

Thomas had to interview prospective workers and contact various tradespeople to keep the business profitable. He was aware that after 1815, the Battle of Waterloo, Napoleon had headed back to France to secure his position, but failed. London rejoiced, especially businesses that had even the smallest connection with the army and the victory, providing weapons, livestock, equipment, flags, celebratory pottery, pictures, jewellery and books. Crowds attended massive celebrations. In the country the harvest began to be gathered in. New inventions, better factories, water power and agricultural improvements all contributed to sweeping changes for workers, after a series of riots and reforms. George III died, at a time when the whole system of government was destined to change. Thomas' walks to see Ester were punctuated by all that was going on. Their life changes accompanied all those national events destined to happen along the way.

He knocked on the door of the shop and Rosie came to open it. "Ester's ready, here she is," she said. Ester came through the doorway out onto the pavement looking every bit his sweetheart.

"Hello my love, it's a lovely day, let's walk," he said. With that they linked arms and proceeded up Queensgate towards Hyde Park Gardens.

He patted his pocket. Yes, the ring was there. They walked over Kensington Gore through Kensington Gate, making for Rotten Row and the Serpentine. It was here that Thomas had decided would be the perfect place to propose, and a seat in the gardens screened by flowing roses was just the job.

"Would you like to stop here for a moment to look at the roses?" he said.

"What a lovely garden," she replied.

Ester propped her parasol against the arm and sat down. Thomas seized the opportunity. "Darling, May I?" Thomas slid off the seat onto one knee. Whilst they had been walking along he had grasped the ring bag, and it was now in his hand. He drew back the drawstring and passed the open bag to Ester. "Ester, will you be mine and marry me?"

"Oh Thomas! You know I will, and yes I will!" With that she tipped the bag into her hand. The ring slid out and the diamond reflected a shaft of sunlight into her face. She let out a loud gasp. "Oh Thomas, it's beautiful!" She tried the ring on her finger. It fitted perfectly.

She began to cry. "Oh Thomas. You will never know what my life has been like. It was so awful to leave home and not have parents with me all these years. The only thing that kept me together was to dream of a beautiful prince who would one day rescue me and never leave me alone again. I know Rosie has been like a mother to me and she's done a wonderful job, but it was never the same, I missed life at home. I pined so much, although I never let on. Now here we are, my dream has been answered, but the reality of being with you is so much better than any dream."

"I too dreamt of a new life," said Thomas. "To find someone like myself who would have similar hopes and fears, someone who would want children, and for them to have the very best start in life that I could give." This brought forth a further tear from Ester.

Thomas explained. "Life in the blacksmith's shop was hard and my church schooling was strict. My parents had difficulty living in Dublin with all the back-biting going on. Ireland's in a mess. Religion has come between the people and the state. But dear Ester, this is a happy day for us both. It is up to us to see that the future will be so too. It's up to us. I would like to think that our marriage will not upset anyone, that we can judge the timing to fit in with both Rose and Josie and my job. But those things are for the future, not today – our engagement day. Today is for you and me, now!"

With that he kissed Ester passionately, at length. Both of them knew that they were going to have to be patient. They were going to have to wait for perhaps years. Their love was strong, but would it be strong enough?

They walked through Kensington Gardens with the flowers in full bloom and the grass looking so green. The band was playing and the soldiers walking their girlfriends gave the occasion a poetry of its own. The couple were lost for words. Their love was embedded deep; it was to have a deep foundation.

Finally they about-turned and made their way back to Drury Lane. It had been a wonderful day which had lived up to all of Thomas' expectations, and he was sure it had matched Ester's. Now they had to tell all those who would be affected by their engagement, and decide on a day to get married. But first things first: they must talk with Rosie and get her opinion and advice.

"Darling, what a lovely walk." Ester was walking in a dream. She had dreamt for so long of this day, and now it had come true. Both of them were in good health. Thomas was earning a good salary and was the general manager of a prosperous company with an excellent reputation. She was now running the shop, having been taught everything Rosie had taught her over many years. They too had a good name and clientele.

"Thomas, during this time before we get married, we should be doing everything to advance our situation."

"What do you mean, my love?"

"Well, I mean collecting furniture, bedclothes, carpets and things."

Thomas thought. "If those things could be stored, that would be wonderful, because it would give us pleasure and a goal to aim for, something to make the wait until we get married more bearable. If we could find a store it's a good idea. I would love it to be possible."

They turned the corner into Queensgate. They would soon be inside, putting all their exciting engagement news and questions to Rosie. They had no fear about discussing anything with her. The door was open, and in they went. Rosie was there.

"Did you have a good walk?" she asked.

Ester took her by the arm. "Look – I'm engaged!" The ring sparkled.

"My, you have been busy!" Rosie laughed. "How lovely. Now come along." She marched into the back room. "Come and sit down and tell me all about it. I can't wait. Did Thomas go down on one knee?"

"Yes he did. He did it exactly how it should be done. It was wonderful. I do so love him."

Thomas shuffled about, embarrassed. "Well I must admit it was a lot easier than I feared. But Ester is a wonderful woman, and she made it easy for me. She accepted with grace and charm, as she always does."

"I'm delighted, and I can see you will be happy. However, things are never that simple. You are talking about making a great change to you lives. This is a moment when you should try and think about how you should behave to ensure the future is as worry-free as you can make it."

"Oh Rosie, you are saying just exactly what we thought you might," said Ester. "You're the first one to know, other than Josie and the jewellery man, and they didn't talk about all the ramifications. We have decided to fit in with your workplace, Thomas' works and Josie's guest house because we don't want to upset anyone, we want to fit in, and be adaptable. We want to keep you all as friends."

"That's very commendable, thank you. Ester, as you know I am all but retired. You are running the shop. If you weren't here I would have to close the shop and sell it. There is the upper floor that has always been unoccupied. Now, would you both like that for the time being, until you are more settled? Perhaps until you start a family. You may decorate and furnish it to your taste and I can set it out legally if you so prefer. That might be appropriate, because if I were to die my relatives would have to abide by how the matter is set up. But that of course is up to you."

"That is very kind of you," said Thomas. "We will give that our closest consideration with pleasure. It's a perfect temporary solution. May we come back to you when I have talked things over with Ester, Mr Bryer and Rosie?"

"Of course, take your time – there's no hurry."

"We are all at sea and excited, not in the best frame of mind to make long-standing decisions. Still, I must get back. May I see you next week and tell you what I find out my end?"

With that Thomas stood up. Ester came over and took his hand, and they walked out of the room towards the front door. Josie called out "Thank you", then turned and kissed Ester. "I love you, dearest Ester." With that he set off once more back to Drury Lane, with a great deal to think about.

On reaching Drury Lane and home, Thomas went up to his room to change for dinner. His visits to Ester and walks back home were now routine. The walk gave him time to digest the how the meeting went and what he had to do before the following Saturday. Now he had to lay the present position on the table before Josie. There was every chance that he would have to leave the guest house to live at the dress shop on the other side of town.

He paused. His last few important years had been spent getting to know the neighbours, becoming familiar with the area around St. Pauls, having his conversations with Josie in her sitting room, all the hard work fitting in at work. It had been a momentous change in life, which he now had become used to – part of his existence. He was going to give it all up to be with the woman he loved, to forge a new life, married and perhaps with children too.

It was now time for dinner. *Oh well, here I go, into the lion's den.* He knew perfectly well that Josie was not going to like what he was going to say, and probably do.

The conversation around the table over dinner highlighted what was happening out in the streets. The Grand Union Canal, built 1801, was used to bring heavy freight into central London, easing the congestion of horse-drawn vehicles on the roads. The Regents Canal helped, delivering new construction materials for housing in north-west London. The impact of the many workers moving down into London to supply labour was felt by everyone. The roads were packed and housing scarce. The conversation flowed backwards and forwards. Every facet of London's society was at full tilt, with entertainment and food shops especially busy.

Eventually the conversation petered out as guests left the table, finally leaving Thomas there alone. Josie came through and tapped him on the shoulder. "Come along. I can tell you're itching to tell me something!"

Thomas took a deep breath. "I offered up the ring and Ester accepted. The day was as perfect as I could ever want. Ester was as delightful as ever. Our talk with Rosie Springer went well. Ester explained that she did not want to leave her in the lurch and that we are not rushing getting married because we wanted to make sure those we love are brought along too, and that if a family were to be created, the children would be given every possible help to grow into well-balanced individuals."

"Well," said Josie, "that all seems sensible, but what about the shop? Doesn't Ester run it for Rosie, and she's about to retire?"

"Yes, but Josie has offered us her top floor rooms to tide us over until she does retire, and until perhaps we can announce a pregnancy. Then we will have to find a home of our own where Ester doesn't have a multitude of stairs to climb."

"My, you do have the future laid out before you! It all sounds fine and I am all for it, although I would like to see you both perhaps for dinner once a month."

Thomas was relieved that Josie was taking the news so well, and dinner once a month sounded perfect.

"I knew you would be happy for us. I'm indebted to you for all your kindnesses. Thank you Josie, I feel much better about it all, now you know and approve. But it's time for bed. It's been a busy day." With that he got up. "Goodnight, my dear Josie," he said, kissing her on the cheek.

CHAPTER 15

Home-making

The following day Thomas rose early. He wanted to plan a new range of celebratory gold brooches and cravat pins and see how they would be moulded to make pouring the gold easier. He needed something to distract him from his thoughts about yesterday, and this delicate job was perfect for doing just that.

It wasn't that Thomas did not look forward to the lead-up to marriage, but he was not so happy to be leaving the guest house which had been his home for so long. However, planning the complete renovation of Rosie's top floor for the use of Ester and himself was exciting, and something he really did wish to plan for perfectly.

His thoughts about moving and planning stayed with

him all week. Saturday came round again, and he took with him a book of plain paper and a pencil. All the way to Queensgate, he thought about what materials they would need. First of all the place had to be swept and then washed down. Now where could he find a sponge?

A knock on the door produced Ester, looking as lovely as ever and dying to kiss him. That he was not going to complain about. "Perhaps we ought to go inside?" she said. Thomas pulled her to him and brushed back her hair. She parted her lips. The kiss was all he needed.

In they went. "Now my darling, we have a task before us. I have never seen the top floor. What about a climb up the stairs to discover our future home?"

They entered the shop and went through the sitting room to mount the stairs to the upper floors. Up they went hand in hand, full of expectations and excitement. At last they came to the third floor landing. From this point on would be theirs for an unknown period, but certainly till Mrs Springer no longer needed it.

"Right my darling. Where do we start?" said Thomas.

Ester boldly went to the further door on the left, opened it and in they went. It was a box room with a window looking out onto the roofs next door. They tried the next room back along the landing, and Ester opened the door. This was obviously the largest room, likely to become their sitting room. It was spacious, and more than enough for them to spread out. The fireplace was the room's central feature, with a mirrored overmantel above. It had great potential to be turned into a really cosy room looking out onto the gardens of houses along the Cromwell Road.

The next room was of similar size, but with an inbuilt fire range that could be perhaps turned into the dining room and the range suitable for heating water for food preparation. There was a window, which would give light even though the ceiling was sloping, being the underside of the roof. Finally they opened the last door, which led to a small room with sloping ceilings.

"I think it has great potential," said Thomas. "I'm a little concerned about water for cooking and washing. We need to visit some shops selling washing implements, furniture and household items to get an idea of what is available."

In the late eighteenth century, water came from wells. Cottages, houses and tenements did not usually have their own well but shared a facility close to, and fetching water for the kitchen, bedroom or toilet was a daily chore. In this instance the water came from a well that was shared. Depending on the underlying rock strata, the water could be many feet below the surface. When dug the water might have come from a own spring, being filtered through mud, shale, pebbles or rock.

After a number of years, depending on the amount of use, the well might become polluted or blocked and had to be dug out. Its cleanliness could not be guaranteed. For drinking or preparing meals, the water had to be boiled. Quite often water or coal for upper floors was raised by a system of ropes over a pulley. Baths were wooden tubs constructed very much like beer barrels.

Until the 19th century a supply of water to individual residences in Britain was still a rare occurrence, although in London the development of sanitation systems was well under way. People would collect water from nearby supplies, which they could then heat up for use as bath water. As industrialisation took place the Saturday night bath became a common occurrence.

People would often have half a day off work on a Saturday, and it commonly ended up being used for the laborious process of getting water, heating it up and filling the bath. Because it took so much work to fill a bath and so long to heat it, the entire family would have to share it.

"Well my dear, what do you think?" said Ester, looking intently at Thomas. "Can we convert these rooms?"

Thomas faltered. "It's going to take a lot of work and I don't want you to overtax yourself. Thankfully we have time to work it out and perhaps get help in for some of the work. We need to look for shops selling washing facilities and rig up a pulley system for fetching the water and coal up."

"Indeed. First the rooms need dusting, sweeping and washing down. Finding a workman to do that should be relatively easy. You will be here to oversee the work and direct operations, and I can come down in the evenings to help out. I'm sure we'll be able to manage. Perhaps there's a local painter and decorator who would undertake the work and give an estimate. On my way back I'll keep my eyes open."

"Let's go downstairs and talk it over with Josie and see what she thinks," said Ester. "We need to assure her that we can manage and not give her any reason to stress or become upset."

"My darling, that is just one of the reasons why I love you so much. You think things through and consider other people's opinions and needs. Yes, you're right, we should go down and talk it through and set her mind at rest."

And that is what they did. Josie was delighted that they had chosen to stay, as it would be company and protection for her. She had often been concerned about the empty rooms upstairs, particularly when the weather was bad. Now that was going to be put right. She went to bed that night pleased with what had been accomplished. The future was being taken care of.

The couple went down to the shop to say their goodbyes, and Thomas put on his topcoat. Ester went to the door. "Good bye, my dear Thomas, take care. I shall be thinking of you." Thomas kissed her and left, striding down Drury Lane. He turned to wave, but she had gone inside.

Back to his thoughts. His mind was taken up with the task to hand, to find a team of house painters who would do the job. His other preoccupation was to look out for possible furnishings and fittings. Already his life had changed, romantic day dreams ousted, to those practical jobs that would create a safe and practical home for his bride to be.

He looked about himself as he walked along. There were

places being repaired and decorated with placards declaring who was doing the job, and one name kept cropping up, Daniel Larking of Thurloe Square. He took notice of the road names. There was a sign to South Kensington, 'local builders, painters and strainers'. Should he go and find this place? Why not take a chance?

He was on the corner of Alexander Square, a large house with adjoining stables. He knocked, and it opened to reveal a large man in paint-splattered dungarees. "Good evening sir, what may I do for you?" he said.

"I'm sorry to disturb you so late in the day. I'm looking for a builder and decorator to refurbish some top floor rooms near Drury Lane."

"Well in that case you'd better come in." The door was flung open wide, and the man stepped aside, beckoning him in. "Now sir. My name is Daniel Larking." He held out his hand and Thomas shook it. "Please excuse me while I get my appointment book."

Thomas looked around. The hall was beautifully kept and the paintwork immaculate.

Back came Mr Larking, flicking through the pages of his book. "Right, I can pop round next Thursday evening at 6.15 if that's convenient."

"That's perfect," said Thomas. "The address is Springers Milliners, Gowns and Suits, 12, Queens Gate Place, off Queensgate."

Mr Larking licked the pencil and repeated the address. "There now, that's fine." With that he snapped the book shut.

"Thank you," said Thomas. "I'll expect you then." With that he stepped back outside, the door held open by Mr Larking. "Next Thursday then. Goodbye." The door closed. Thomas made his way back to the Brompton Road, to continue his journey back home to Drury Lane and dinner, his mind full of pieces of furniture and the colours of walls.

Thursday soon came round. Thomas had explained about Mr Larking and his business to both Rosie and Ester, emphasising the perfection of the work he had seen and assuring them that Mr Larking would do a good job.

At six-thirty a knock came on the shop door. Rosie opened it to be confronted by Mr Larking, with a cheery "Good evening madam, sorry I'm late, wasn't too sure how to get here."

"Don't worry Mr Larking, please come in," she replied. "Thomas has explained about your visit. Perhaps you would like to come upstairs and see what we are talking about."

"I'd be delighted, please lead the way." With that the four of them made their way up the stairs to the top floor. Thomas stepped forward and shook Daniel's hand. "Right, let's start here." He opened the door to the smallest room. Mr Larking opened his book and made a simple drawing of the room, adding the approximate sizes of the interior.

"Right, perhaps you could describe how you would like me to decorate this" he said. "What colours you would like used and if the floor is to be carpeted, and possibly what the room will be used for. However, before you start, may I suggest that your refurbishment designs includes the landing, to keep the whole floor sympathetic, to tie in each room with the landing? Rest assured, nothing will be done until all the surfaces have been properly prepared."

"This is going to be the spare room for luggage, cases, etc.," said Thomas. "However, we would like the room to contain a fitted boxed toilet pan."

The colour scheme for the whole floor was agreed as a light pale yellow-cream with pale pink woodwork. Thomas walked across to the next room, planned to be their sitting room, and Mr Larking carried out the same procedure, making a plan and entering the dimensions. Next the bedroom, which was also to serve as the washing and bathing room. The small room on the right was for hanging clothes.

"I think I have all the information necessary for an estimate to be made," said Mr Larking. "May I drop it in sometime tomorrow? I will make it as reasonable as possible. If you agree with the basic price, please would you sign it and let me have it as soon as possible. Building the cupboards and toilet seat container will be done by my joiner."

Ester and Thomas thanked him for his trouble. The estimate was made and all three agreed it was a fair price. Rosie insisted that she would pay the bill and would not take no for an answer. Thomas dropped in the signed estimate to Mr Larking, who said that he would start the following week. He believed the whole job would take about a fortnight, giving the washing-down time to dry.

It was an exciting time for Ester and Thomas. As the work progressed, they could not stop themselves visiting the upstairs floor to see each day's progress. This was to be their first home, planned by them and furnished by them, every part carefully chosen by both.

The fortnight sped by, and at last they could mount the stairs to see the finished work. They looked at each other, kissed and opened the door to their bedroom. The pale yellow walls and ceiling, white cornice, and the dusty pink door frame, dado, skirting and plate rack were all perfectly picked out. They stood there and drew breath. They were looking at the place where they would lie together as man and wife.

"Darling Ester, this is ours, for me, and I expect for you also. A dream that has repeated itself in hard, lonely times. I have been through many of those, but they are all surpassed by this moment, of you, my love, being by my side, in my arms, kissing and caressing me." Tears came into his eyes. She kissed them away.

"I know, I was there with you, always," she said.

CHAPTER 16

A home of their own

Now that their rooms were ready, they had to furnish them in such a way that they could be used in future homes too. The most important items were the bed, settee, sideboard, dressing table and dining table and chairs. Thomas had to provide certain metal fitments for Thomas Tennant, Household Furniture Maker, warehoused in Long Lane. He also sold to Surman's Great House, Soho. He told Ester he would see Mr Tennant about some furniture. It was likely that he could get a good price reduction from him because W. Bryer & Sons made fitments for some of his furniture.

The next day Thomas walked round to Thomas Tennant's to see what was available, keeping the list firmly in his mind. He was going to pay for the furniture which would be both Thomas' and Esters' for life, and hopefully then passed down. He went straight into the warehouse office, where Thomas was working on a new design.

"Hello Thomas, good to see you looking so well. Not often you're round here, you must want something?"

"Well, since you put it like that, yes I do. I want some furniture for my new home." Thomas went on to tell his friend all about Ester and the proposed wedding, how his new home was taking shape and the furniture he was looking for. Tennant congratulated him, saying he was a lucky devil, as his warehouse was stocked full for the winter season and he could let him have a few excess items from the previous year far cheaper, to give him more room for this year's stock.

"Here, write down what you're looking for and I'll see what I can do," he said. "Can I deliver them? If so to where?" Thomas gave him the address. "Right, that's not too far away, I'll do my best. I'll drop off the invoice at the same time. How will that do you?"

"Mr Tennant, you're a star, shining ever brighter, thank the Lord. That will be just fine."

Thomas walked back to Aldersgate, please that he had thought about his old friend Thomas Tennant. The furniture from Tennant's was very high class. He could rely upon his friend. Now all that was required were carpets, curtains, bed linen and blankets. All were in Ester's domain of knowledge and present business connections.

He met up with Ester the same evening. His story about

ordering the furniture excited her. He explained that she would have to face Thomas Tennant's delivery men the next day and direct operations to have the furniture lifted up the stairs onto the top floor, making sure the removal men didn't damage the wood or paintwork.

When Thomas left Ester that evening, she had agreed to contact local suppliers of material for the curtains and the makers of ready-made sheets, pillow cases and blankets. The bedspread might have to be provided by a specialist, depending on its design, but it could wait. The manufacturers who supplied the shop or others that supplied the trade might have samples they could select from.

It took six weeks to finally have the top floor just as they had planned. The whole was painted and decorated, cupboards built and positioned, curtains hung, floor coverings laid and bed made up. It had cost nearly all of Thomas' hard-earned savings, plus the kindness of Josie, who insisted on paying her share.

The bracket had been bolted in above the window, a pulley hung and a rope fed through. There were buckets for fresh water, waste water and coal, including firewood. Thomas and Ester had practised many times with each item to get the heavy buckets in though the two open windows that were specially designed to open back and come together. The fire-stove in the sitting-room had to cook the meals, heat the water and provide heating. The coal cupboard had to be kept topped up throughout the year, so the fire was hardly ever out. The bathing tub stood behind the drawn curtains. The commode, the boxed-in cistern, built in the smallest lumber room had its own washbasin and towels. Their top-floor apartment had all the latest labour-saving devices designed and displayed in the latest fashion.

A bathroom of the period, showing commode

It was now almost six years since Thomas had travelled to London, started work at Sirrells' and transferred to William Bryer's. He had met Ester, his now constant companion, become engaged, and found a new home for them both in Rosie Springer's top-floor apartment. This had been renovated and decorated for their future, as it was to be their home until a child was born and settled, ready to be moved to a new permanent home, one fit to bring up a family. Before this however, the couple were to have the banns called to be married.

It was the late summer of 1818. They were moving in

unmarried, having previously decided not to consummate their relationship until after marriage. Their kind friends Rosie Springer and Josie Whitehouse were aware what the couple's intentions were, as were Thomas' parents. They had waited patiently for the right moment, knowing that afterwards life would never be the same. In many respects the lives they had known before, Thomas closely experiencing the darker side of Dublin's city life, the slums and waterfront squalor, and Ester's proximity to neighbouring children whose parents were poor and took their battles with life out on their children, made them grateful and appreciative of what they had and what they were planning to do.

Thomas and Ester had talked and planned endlessly about how they were going to prepare for marriage and look after each other. Tonight they were going to sleep together for the first time. They had only kissed and petted, withholding any kind of physical relationship and keeping that for another occasion, which was now upon them. You might believe they were prudish, unfeeling and unromantic; you would be wrong. The couple were nervous, but that was to be expected. Certainly they were excited, and of course longing to be forever closer and touching, kissing and caressing.

It was nine o'clock, and Ester had come upstairs prepared to go to bed. Removing her shoes, she washed in their little wash-room, and she sat on the bed. All her thoughts quickly traversed through home, her the lonely coach journey, the introduction to Rosie, becoming trained, meeting Thomas, forging their engagement and their planned vision to build their future home together.

Now here she sat, fiddling with her bodice, letting down her hair. She stood and slipped off her clothes, gently folding them into a neat pile and placing them on the chair. Standing naked, she slipped into her nightdress, purposely leaving the bodice untied, then lay on the bed, and pulled the sheet around her, just a second before Thomas came in through the door.

"Nearly caught you," he said. "My goodness, you look beautiful."

She chuckled and turned on her side momentarily sliding one leg out. Softly she said, "Now it's your turn to undress – come along now, I'm waiting!

Thomas needed no urging, but his own pile of clothes was nowhere near so neat! He turned his back as he donned his nightshirt. Then he turned and gently climbed into the bed.

They lay there looking at each other. Ester smiled. "My darling, what a journey we've had to make to reach this moment. I hope it lasts forever. I am yours, I want you to love me and share this moment, for I have thought of little else, but this moment, since meeting you." "Darling Ester the same goes for me. Please guide me, let me know if I am hurting you in any way – be my guardian in love."

Both Thomas and Ester were thoughtful people both relatively old to be married for the first time. Thomas was 28 and Ester 25. They appreciated how lucky they were and how sympathetic and understanding to their past life – leaving their homes and loved ones, to make a life on their own. They knew it was up to each of them to be kind and thoughtful, and to try not to allow any mishaps, difficulties, or embarrassments to occur; knowing their future life was tied up with this critical moment, how their first night's love-making would seal and improve their mutual love for each other.

They were no different from any other couple entering the marital bed for the first time. Others had been there by chance, or by design, perhaps during relationships that had not lasted. However, in this case, and for many others, both knew this was to be for the first time and neither wanted to spoil the occasion, nor to be crude or unfeeling towards the other. Their love was more mature and considerate, by mutual consent. However, there is always a first time. They had both talked though about having children, and knew that what they were about to do could lead to their first child, changing their lives forever. Mentally and materially. they were prepared. There was no turning back; the die was cast. Thomas knelt before his dearest...

They lay there looking at each other. Ester smiled. "Well Thomas, here I am, all yours."

"So you are, and I am yours," said Thomas. He touched her face and kissed her forehead gently, taking his time, treasuring every second.

They giggled and snuggled down, their bodies touching. They were each intoxicated by the other's nearness. Now for the first time, shyness had been removed, and they could touch and kiss each other whenever they wanted.

On many Saturday afternoons they had visited many galleries and museums, and seen pictures and sculptures of the perfect human form. They had both taken note of their opposite's features and forms relishing the thought of seeing each other without clothes. Thomas could not resist the pure delight of looking down at Ester's body. He touched her stomach, and she placed her hand on his, "Oh darling!" she murmured. She smiled and snuggled into his body and he took her in his arms.

Their joint final thoughts before sleep were that their love was complete at last.

They woke the next morning still in an embrace. "Morning, my dearest." Thomas smiled and kissed her. "Work is going to be horribly boring after last night. But we have all our lives ahead. You'll get very bored with me!"

"I'm willing to bet on that!" said Ester, smiling. Now they both had to resume their previous daily lives and to eagerly look forward to their evenings together. There was a wedding to save and plan for.

As the weeks slid by, their lives together changed, but the thrill of sleeping together never left them. Their closeness and care for each other would last for ever. Rosie commented on their remarkable closeness, and was told that having to leave home had cemented their desire to stay together forever, whatever trials and tribulations life was to throw up. And they did.

Over time Rosie was increasingly unable to walk and became bed-bound, but in Ester's hands the business, flourished allowing her to have a live-in helper until the doctors gave her only a few more weeks to live. Both Thomas and Ester knew that Rosie's will left her estate to a distant relative.

Just after Christmas 1818, Ester and Thomas decided to start a family and to seek a permanent home. They immediately approached the vicar of St. Thomas' Church Soho, who agreed to call the banns for a wedding later in the year. Meanwhile the pair had to inform their parents and friends what was afoot so that they could firm up a date, eventually setting a date of 17th October 1819.

St. Mary's Church, Soho, Westminster, 1819

The Goldsmiths' Hall was booked, and the catering was organised by Josie Whitehouse as a wedding present. Steven James contributed the wine. There were only twenty invited to the reception, which took place in a small room off the main hall. Rosie and Ester made sure the table was finely furnished with flowers and seat settings. As the hall was so near to the guesthouse, the food was prepared there and carried to a table which had been set aside for the servers to use. The occasion was a happy affair, and the guests all praised the efforts of both Josie and Rose with many salutations. At last the happy couple departed, taking a special coach home to Queensgate. They made their way up the stairs, holding hands. They were devoted to each other, and never forgot their wonderful life together at Drury Lane.

Ester became pregnant shortly afterwards. Life would never be the same again. Thomas, their first son, first saw the light of day on the 24th July, 1820. A new permanent home now had to be found. Rosie had sold the business and was expected to live with her relatives, as Rosie had wanted. It was exciting for the pair, a new first baby, looking for a home, and finding a new part of London to live in, closer to all the conveniences a family would need.

Thomas Smith of Chelsea began building in Earl's Court in 1803-5, and by 1819 he had built two large houses and a number of smaller houses in Earl's Court Road north of Kenway. Finally he bought land from Coles Smith, building houses off Redfield Lane and Wallgrave Road. North Row was south of West Cromwell Road, Earls Court, part of 'Old Brompton' Kensington, and not far from today's Earls Court Station. Close to Cromwell Road, 20 North Row was empty. This was to be the home in which Ester and Thomas would live out their days, bringing up a family of seven children. Following Thomas came Esther (1822), Mary (1823), Charlotte (1828), Elizabeth (1831), William

(1837) and Emma (1839). Thomas and Ester were united in love which lasted to their dying day.

The Kearey Clan

My writings about the family, particularly their revelations of the strong connection with Ireland, have been a talking point throughout the family. With that in mind a suggestion to apply for Grant of Arms has stirred up even more interest, particularly now since the Irish Herald has accepted and recommended that the application should proceed in my favour. The Grant of Arms is to be based upon my descent from Thomas Kearey, who appears in the 1851 census records as married to Ester Pepler, residents at 20 North Row in Kensington. His description as having been born in Ireland renders me eligible. The Herald goes on to say that from a heraldic point of view the Grant of Arms may make reference to the generally accepted origin of the name in the Irish word 'Ciar', combining this with heraldic devices that may tell a story of my own immediate family starting with Thomas, born in 1791, and in that way including the family arms in the wider context of the name. The inspiration for a newly-created coat of arms may be drawn from a variety of different sources where there is no clear pronominal coat of arms of the name with which one can clearly prove an association. Elements may reflect certain biological details of the grantee, his or her origin, interests, occupation or ideals. In the devisal of arms it is rarely possible to make more than two or three references without producing a cluttered shield, and good armory is almost invariably simple.

A preliminary sketch utilises the smith's hammers shown in chief (uppermost) in the shield above what is known as a fess wavy. This wavy element is intended to reference the Thames and the hammers located above the wavy (or undé) element a reference to my ancestor's residence over generations north of the Thames. The chief section of the shield is Sable (black) as a reference to the origin of the Kearey name in the Irish language 'ciar' (dark) while the hammers are Argent (silver) as a sharp contrast to the black and the reference to my ancestor's work with silver and gold smelting. In a similar way, the use of both silver (argent) in the central 'wave' and gold in the base of the shield is a reference to the family's past association with silver and gold smelting.

My father's contribution, together with other members of the family, to the First World War, especially his connection to the Kensington regiment, making a link with a number of resident's houses in the borough, can be included in the arms. For discussion it was suggested a crest (wreath) on top of a closed helmet seen in profile with a hand and arm vambraced couped, holding a bayonet with four fingers or clenched proper raised to indicate the four brothers lost on the First World War.

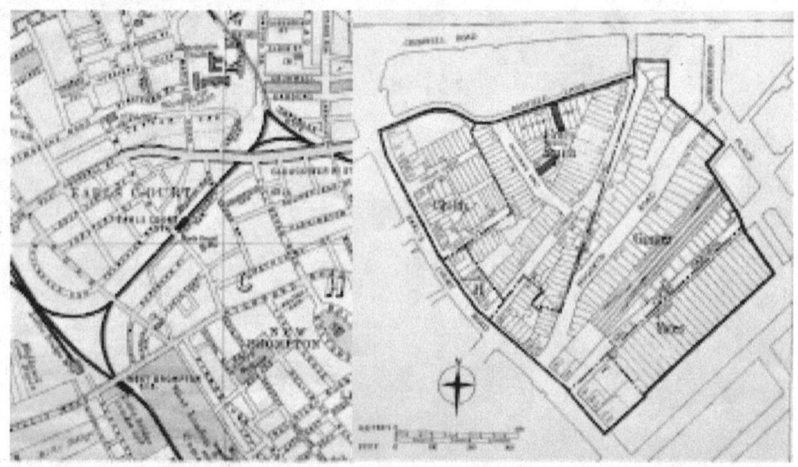

Thomas and Ester's son Thomas and wife Hannah lived in Earls Court, close to Hogarth Road.

www.ingramcontent.com/pod-product-compliance
Lightning Source LLC
LaVergne TN
LVHW030921080826
845145LV00013B/3000
9781861518194